If anyone out there is reading this, I need your help. I am trapped within a really terrible Dungeons and Dragons campaign and I can't find my way out. My player is a horny 14-year-old loser who won't stop forcing me to have sex with slutty elf chicks instead of going on quests. The Dungeon Master has severe Attention Deficit Disorder and skips large sections of description when it comes to the world I live within. Please find my character sheet and bring it to a better Dungeon Master, preferably a benevolent one with a vivid imagination who actually knows what he's doing. Please, I beg of you to deliver me from this nightmare, before all of my hit points run out . . .

- Polo Pipefingers, level 3 Halfling Fighter

THE KOBOLD WIZARD'S DILDO
OF ENLIGHTENMENT +2

Also by Carlton Mellick III

Satan Burger
Electric Jesus Corpse
Sunset With a Beard (stories)
Razor Wire Pubic Hair
Teeth and Tongue Landscape
The Steel Breakfast Era
The Baby Jesus Butt Plug
Fishy-fleshed
The Menstruating Mall
Ocean of Lard (with Kevin L. Donihe)
Punk Land
Sex and Death in Television Town
Sea of the Patchwork Cats
The Haunted Vagina
Cancer-cute (Avant Punk Army Exclusive)
War Slut
Sausagey Santa
Ugly Heaven, Beautiful Hell (with Jeffrey Thomas)
Adolf in Wonderland
Ultra Fuckers
Cybernetrix
The Egg Man
Apeshit
The Faggiest Vampire
The Cannibals of Candyland
Warrior Wolf Women of the Wasteland

DUNGEON MODULE B69

THE KOBOLD WIZARD'S DILDO OF ENLIGHTENMENT +2

AN ADVENTURE FOR 3-6 PLAYERS, LEVELS 2-5

CARLTON MELLICK III

AVANT PUNK

AVANT PUNK

AN IMPRINT OF ERASERHEAD PRESS

ERASERHEAD PRESS
205 NE BRYANT
PORTLAND, OR 97211

WWW.ERASERHEADPRESS.COM

ISBN: 1-936383-05-5

Printed in the USA.

TABLE OF CONTENTS

CHARTS AND REFERENCES

saturday night is dungeons and dragons night

DM NOTE

When I was a kid, I had to make a very tough decision. I had to choose between my two biggest obsessions and decide once and for all which one of them I would dedicate my life to:

A) Writing books.
or
B) Playing DUNGEONS AND FUCKING DRAGONS!

I chose A, of course, but let me tell you something: I totally fucked up. I should have chosen Dungeons and Dragons. I mean writing books is fine and all, but nothing beats a good night of D&D. Nothing is more satisfying than leveling up your half-elf ranger after surviving a particularly challenging dragon battle, with over half of your party killed off, leaving most of the treasure to you and your nearly-dead dwarf thief friend who only survived because he used his "hide in shadows" ability for practically the whole goddamned quest. Now that is what I call glory. That is what life is all about. But no, I had to be a fucking dumbass and choose writing. It's still a cool gig, but if I could have somehow made a living off of playing Dungeons and Dragons professionally I totally would have done that instead.

It's funny but I believe that I actually learned more about how to write from Dungeon Mastering than I did from taking creative writing classes. I think it is because when you create stories for Dungeons and Dragons, you have to consider your audience. You're not taught to consider your audience in creative writing classes. You are taught to express yourself or how to intelligently work subtext into your story. They don't teach you how to keep your audience interested and engaged. They don't teach you how not to be boring. When you've created a shitty quest as a DM, your players let you know. They might not say it to your face, but once they start yawning, going home early, and making excuses not to come to the next week's session, you know you've fucked up. So if you happen to be a writer and think you're wasting your time playing D&D, you should remember that you can learn a lot from playing Dungeons and Dragons. Not only did it help me with storytelling, but also worldbuilding, characterization, and even illustration. To tell you the truth, pretty much all of my art skills originated from years of illustrating the profile pics on character sheets.

This book is dedicated to the years of my life when I was most obsessed with D&D (12-14). It is also dedicated to all of my friends I have played D&D with over the years: Aaron Donnelly (who was Mormon and always played the wizard), Daniel Donnelly (who was a hyperactive kid who loved to destroy things and talk about boners), Jason Meador (my best friend when I was 14, who was sensitive about his height and totally into Satan), Josh Webb (my first DM in 5th grade), Vince Kramer (who got me back into D&D for a couple months when I was 19), and Buzz Jepson (the Trekkie kid I used to play chess with at lunch when I was 15).

So, you hold in your hands *The Kobold Wizard's Dildo of Enlightenment +2*, which was originally titled *The Eyeball Wizard's Toy Cunt* back when it was only in the outlining stages about 6 years ago. Now I do have to say that this is the stupidest book I have ever written. I say that a lot these days, but this time I really mean it. If there exists another book with this many boners in it I would be completely amazed. But, you know, when you are writing a book set in a world that has been created by 12-14 year old nerds there is going to be a hell of a lot of boners in it. Still, I might have gone a little bit overboard on this one. I hope you enjoy it anyway.

- Carlton Mellick III
06/01/10 7:24 pm

P.S. - Make sure to cut out the character sheets, npc sheets, and especially the maps from this book and keep them with you while reading the story. That way you can follow the characters on the map and change their stats as they lose hit points, etc. This is the way the book was intended to be read.

character sheets

Player's Name:	
Mark Meador	

Character's Name:
Polo Pipe-fingers

Race:
Halfling

Class:
Fighter

Level: 3

Alignment:
Neutral Good

THAC0: 17

Height: 3'4 **Age:** 29

Weight: 69 lbs **Sex:** M

Hair: brown **Eyes:** brown

HIT POINTS	ARMOR CLASS
24 / 24	5 / 4

ATTRIBUTES

	Attack Adj.	Damage Adj.	Weight Allow	Open Doors	BB/LG
STR 12	0	0	45	6	4%

	Reaction Adj.	Defense Adj.	Move Silently	Hide in shadows
DEX 8	0	0	X	X

	Hit Points Adj.	Shock Survival	Resurrection Survival
CON 17	+3	97%	98%

	Languages	Learn Spell Chance	# of Spells Per Lvl
INT 10	+2	X	X

	Magic Attack Adj.	Spell Bonus	Chance of Spell Failure
WIS 16	+2	X	X

	Max # henchmen	Loyalty Base	Reaction Adj.
CHA 11	4	normal	normal

		current xp	xp for next lvl
Experience Points:		4,321	8,000

SKILLS

Halfling skills (+4 on saving throws vs wands, spells, and poisons, infravision 30', 50% direction sense, sneak/surprise 66%, +1 to hit with slings/thrown weapons), Secondary skills: forestry, sense motive, handle animals, and forgery.

EQUIPMENT

Chainmail, small shield, short sword +1 (1d6+1), sling (1d4), bag of holding, rations x5, 50' rope, waterskin, 4 torches, dildo of enlightenment +2

GP: 0

HISTORY

Polo Pipe-fingers was given his name because he always had a pipe in his hands, smoking clove-flavored tobacco. After the skin around his eyes turned a shade of black due to clove smoke, he decided to give up smoking. He tried to get his earned name changed after that, but once a halfling's name is earned it sticks with them for the rest of their life. Polo took up adventuring to get away from his mom, because she was a total bitch.

LANGUAGES

Common, dwarven, elven, gnomish, goblinese, orcish

Player's Name: Buzz Jepson	
Character's Name: Delvok	
Race: Elf	
Class: Ranger/Cleric/Mage/Fighter	
Level: 1/1/1/1	
Alignment: Lawful Neutral	
THAC0: 20	
Height: 5'4 **Age:** 127	
Weight: 137 lbs **Sex:** M	
Hair: black **Eyes:** green	

HIT POINTS	ARMOR CLASS
6 / 6	6

ATTRIBUTES

	Attack Adj.	Damage Adj.	Weight Allow	Open Doors	BB/LG
STR 13	0	0	45	7	4%

	Reaction Adj.	Defense Adj.	Move Silently	Hide in shadows
DEX 14	0	0	X	X

	Hit Points Adj.	Shock Survival	Resurrection Survival
CON 14	0	88%	92%

	Languages	Learn Spell Chance	# of Spells Per Lvl
INT 13	+ 3	55%	9

	Magic Attack Adj.	Spell Bonus	Chance of Spell Failure
WIS 14	0	1st	X

	Max # henchmen	Loyalty Base	Reaction Adj.
CHA 11	4	normal	normal

	current xp	xp for next lvl
Experience Points:	1,150 /	1500/2000/2250/2500

cut along the dotted line

SKILLS

Elf skills: 90% resist sleep/charm magic, 60' infravision, find secret doors. Wizard spells: sleep, Priest spells: cure light wounds, bless. Turn undead, hunting.

EQUIPMENT

Scalemail, cloak, holy symbol, 2 vials of holy water, long sword (1d8), long bow (1d6), quiver of 20 arrows, backpack, rations, waterskin, spell book, 50' rope.

GP: 0

HISTORY

Delvok has always been known as the most intelligent, respected, and logical elf from his clan. He believes in logic and reason, but has no need for illogical human emotions. He spends his free time only on intellectual pursuits, because he finds wasting time on relaxation and mindless entertainment highly illogical. Most people he encounters are incredibly jealous of his genius.

LANGUAGES

Common, elven, gnomish, orcish

Player's Name: Todd Donnelly					
Character's Name: The Dwarf Lord					
Race: Dwarf					
Class: Barbarian					
Level: 4					
Alignment: Chaotic Neutral					
THAC0: 16					
Height: 4'1 **Age:** 59					
Weight: 160 lbs **Sex:** M					
Hair: red **Eyes:** blue					

HIT POINTS	ARMOR CLASS
37 / 37	8

ATTRIBUTES

	Attack Adj.	Damage Adj.	Weight Allow	Open Doors	BB/LG
STR 17	+1	+1	85	10	13%

	Reaction Adj.	Defense Adj.	Move Silently	Hide in shadows	
DEX 13	0	0	X	X	

	Hit Points Adj.	Shock Survival	Resurrection Survival	
CON 16	+2	95%	96%	

	Languages	Learn Spell Chance	# of Spells Per Lvl	
INT 9	+2	X	X	

	Magic Attack Adj.	Spell Bonus	Chance of Spell Failure	
WIS 4	-2	X	X	

	Max # henchmen	Loyalty Base	Reaction Adj.	
CHA 9	4	normal	normal	

	current xp	xp for next lvl
Experience Points:	8,231 / 16,000	

SKILLS

Dwarf skills (+6 on saving throws vs wands, spells, and poisons, infravision 60', 50% detect traps, 75% detect slopes, new construction), Barbarian abilities: berserker rage, terrain navigation,tracking, shelter, climb nature, surprise. Secondary skills: leather working, butt sex.

EQUIPMENT

Leather Armor, battleaxe (1d8), backpack, rations, 50' rope, lantern, oil, waterskin.

GP: 1,865

HISTORY

The dwarf lord is fucking bad ass! He's the ruler of all dwarves and can beat the crap out of just about anyone! One time, he cut the heads off of about thirty dragons all at the same time! Then he defeated an army of kobolds or some other race that's tougher than kobolds and he did it all by himself! If you think you're tougher then The Dwarf Lord then you are fucking stupid!

LANGUAGES

Common, dwarven, orcish

Cut along the dotted line

Player's Name:	
Jennifer Donnelly	
Character's Name:	
Robyn Woodsong	
Race:	
Human	
Class:	
Bard	
Level: 1	
Alignment:	
Lawful Good	
THAC0: 20	
Height: 6'0 **Age:** 19	
Weight: 142 lbs **Sex:** F	
Hair: blonde **Eyes:** green	

HIT POINTS	**ARMOR CLASS**
4 / 4	8

ATTRIBUTES

STR 11	Attack Adj.	Damage Adj.	Weight Allow	Open Doors	BB/LG
	0	0	40	6	2%

DEX 15	Reaction Adj.	Defense Adj.	Move Silently	Hide in shadows
	0	-1	X	X

CON 6	Hit Points Adj.	Shock Survival	Resurrection Survival
	-1	50%	55%

INT 15	Languages	Learn Spell Chance	# of Spells Per Lvl
	+4	X	X

WIS 7	Magic Attack Adj.	Spell Bonus	Chance of Spell Failure
	-1	X	X

CHA 18	Max # henchmen	Loyalty Base	Reaction Adj.
	15	+8	+7

Experience Points:	current xp	xp for next lvl
	0 /	1,250

SKILLS

Singing, musical instrument (lute), inspire and influence with music (+1 to attacks), charm person 10%, 15% pick poclets. 25% detect noise, 70% climb walls, 10% read languages.

EQUIPMENT

lute, long sword (1d8), cloak, leather armor, rations, dagger (1d4), waterskin, 10 torchers, large sack

GP: 50

HISTORY

Robyn is a pretty magical singing princess that everyone loves and is always nice to because she is the best singer and most beautiful of everyone in the world and she is also best friends with fairies and mermaids and unicorns and lives in a castle with magical pink swimming pools and has fairy ballroom dances with handsome princes who are always nice and never call her ugly.

LANGUAGES

common, human, elven, halfling, pixie

npc sheets

Player's Name:	
NPC	
Character's Name:	
Loxi Toa	
Race:	
Elf	
Class:	
Assassin	
Level: 4	
Alignment:	
Neutral Evil	
THAC0: 17	

Height: 5'1 **Age:** 134

Weight: 121 lbs **Sex:** F

Hair: green **Eyes:** gold

HIT POINTS	ARMOR CLASS
16 / 16	5

ATTRIBUTES

STR 15	Attack Adj. 0	Damage Adj. 0	Weight Allow 55	Open Doors 8	BB/LG 7%
DEX 16	Reaction Adj. +1	Defense Adj. -2	Move Silently X	Hide in shadows X	
CON 10	Hit Points Adj. 0	Shock Survival 70%	Resurrection Survival 75%		
INT 11	Languages + 2	Learn Spell Chance X	# of Spells Per Lvl X		
WIS 10	Magic Attack Adj. X	Spell Bonus X	Chance of Spell Failure X		
CHA 8	Max # henchmen 3	Loyalty Base -1	Reaction Adj. normal		

	current xp	xp for next lvl
Experience Points:	6,500	/ 12,000

cut along the dotted line

SKILLS

Class skills: Assassination, backstab, hide in shadows
40%, Detect Noise 15%, Climb Walls 70%, Pick Pock-
ets 30%, open locks 20%, find/remove traps 5%, move
silently 45%. Elf skills: 90% resist sleep/charm magic,
60' infravision, find secret doors. Secondary skills:
barter skill.

EQUIPMENT

2 broad swords (1d8), clothes, 2 daggers (1d4), vial
of poison, bullet belt of protection +3, vial of poison,
thieves tools, rations, waterskin, small sack.
GP: 2,120

HISTORY

Loxi comes from a long line of seductive elf assassins
that use their powers of attraction to rob, manipu-
late, and murder members of the opposite sex. Loxi
has no family and has never cared about another
living being outside of her lover and traveling com-
panion, Juzii Alon. Although sex and murder are her
favorite pastimes, she also enjoys knitting, dancing,
and making fun of fat people.

LANGUAGES

Common, elven, gnomish, orcish

Player's Name:	
NPC	

Player's Name: NPC	
Character's Name: Juzii Alon	
Race: Elf	
Class: Illusionist/Thief	
Level: 2/3	
Alignment: Neutral Evil	
THAC0: 19	
Height: 4'11 **Age:** 122	
Weight: 106 lbs **Sex:** F	
Hair: purple **Eyes:** blue	

HIT POINTS	ARMOR CLASS
12 / 12	7

ATTRIBUTES

		Attack Adj.	Damage Adj.	Weight Allow	Open Doors	BB/LG
STR	**7**	-1	0	20	1	0%

		Reaction Adj.	Defense Adj.	Move Silently	Hide in shadows
DEX	**15**	0	-1	X	X

		Hit Points Adj.	Shock Survival	Resurrection Survival
CON	**6**	-1	97%	98%

		Languages	Learn Spell Chance	# of Spells Per Lvl
INT	**14**	+ 4	60%	9

		Magic Attack Adj.	Spell Bonus	Chance of Spell Failure
WIS	**13**	0	1st	X

		Max # henchmen	Loyalty Base	Reaction Adj.
CHA	**13**	5	normal	+1

	current xp	xp for next lvl
Experience Points:	2900 /	4500/5000

SKILLS

Elf skills: 90% resist sleep/charm magic, 60' infravision, find secret doors. Thief skills: pick pockets 45%, open locks 10%, find/remove traps 5%, move silently 45%, hide in shadows 40%, detect noise 20%, climb walls 70%, backstab +4 damage x2. Illusionist spells: change self, hypnotism. Secondary skills: painting, prostition.

EQUIPMENT

Leather armor, small sack, 8 darts, short sword (1d6), dagger (1d4), aviator goggles of protection +2, rations, spell book, thieves tools.

GP: 795

HISTORY

In her youth, Juzii was outcast from her elf clan for being a serial rapist who preyed on young human men. All alone in the world, she took up prostitution as a career for several years until she fell in love with her favorite client, Loxi Toa. She then went into business as a freelance thief and travelled the world with Loxi, searching for gullible adventurers that could easily be robbed, killed, and/or raped.

LANGUAGES

Common, halfling, elven, gnomish, dwarven

Player's Name: NPC		
Character's Name: Glimworm		
Race: Kobold		
Class: Mage		
Level: 9		
Alignment: True Neutral		
THAC0: 19		
Height: 3'3 **Age:** 43		
Weight: 64 lbs **Sex:** M		
Hair: x **Eyes:** black		

HIT POINTS	ARMOR CLASS
28 / 28	7

ATTRIBUTES

	Attack Adj.	Damage Adj.	Weight Allow	Open Doors	BB/LG
STR 12	0	0	45	6	4%

	Reaction Adj.	Defense Adj.	Move Silently	Hide in shadows	
DEX 8	0	0	X	X	

	Hit Points Adj.	Shock Survival	Resurrection Survival	
CON 17	+3	97%	98%	

	Languages	Learn Spell Chance	# of Spells Per Lvl	
INT 16	+5	65%	11	

	Magic Attack Adj.	Spell Bonus	Chance of Spell Failure	
WIS 16	+2	2nd	X	

	Max # henchmen	Loyalty Base	Reaction Adj.	
CHA 11	4	normal	normal	

	current xp	xp for next lvl
Experience Points:	250,400 /	375,000

cut along the dotted line

SKILLS

Wizard spells 1st: magic missile, identify, light, sleep,
2nd: detect invisibility, locate object, knock, strength
3rd: fireball, clairvoyance, hold person. 4th: ice storm,
massmorph

EQUIPMENT

wizard robe, ring of protection + 3, large sack, spell
book, dagger (1d4), staff (1d6), scrolls of read lan-
guages, invisibility, and protection from evil.
GP: 18,500

HISTORY

Glimworm is a collector of ancient artifacts and lives in the
highest tower in Bakerton. He is the only kobold allowed in
the city due to his civilized personality and heavy wallet. As
a child, he was sold into slavery by his own clan and was pur-
chased by an elven sorcerer who saw potential in the young
kobold. After a few years of servitude, Glimworm was even-
tually made an apprentice of the sorcerer and one day be-
come a powerful mage, respected throughout the land.

LANGUAGES

Common, kobold, ogre, trollish, dwarven, elven, gnom-
ish, halfling, orcish

cut along the dotted line

Player's Name:	
NPC	

Player's Name:
NPC

Character's Name:
King Gnoryc

Race:
Gnoll

Class:
Fighter

Level: 5

Alignment:
Neutral Evil

THAC0: 16

Height: 8'2 **Age:** 31

Weight: 259 lbs **Sex:** M

Hair: brown **Eyes:** brown

HIT POINTS	ARMOR CLASS
35 / 35	3

ATTRIBUTES

STR 17	Attack Adj.	Damage Adj.	Weight Allow	Open Doors	BB/LG
	+1	+1	85	10	13%

DEX 14	Reaction Adj.	Defense Adj.	Move Silently	Hide in shadows	
	O	O	X	X	

CON 17	Hit Points Adj.	Shock Survival		Resurrection Survival	
	+3	97%		98%	

INT 10	Languages	Learn Spell Chance		# of Spells Per Lvl	
	+1	X		X	

WIS 10	Magic Attack Adj.	Spell Bonus		Chance of Spell Failure	
	O	X		X	

CHA 13	Max # henchmen	Loyalty Base		Reaction Adj.	
	5	normal		+1	

Experience Points:	current xp	xp for next lvl
	9,000 /	35,000

SKILLS

wolf taming, hunting, sexual stamina, leadership

EQUIPMENT

Platemail, small shield, two-handed sword (1d10),
short sword +2 (1d6+2), wineskin, pantyhose

GP: 1200

HISTORY

Gnoryc is the toughest, most brutal gnoll in the region.
His army has been raping and pillaging the lands out-
side of Bakerton for several years now, but no war-
rior sent to dispatch them has ever stood a chance.
Recently, his army has taken over the hidden keep of
Tardis to act as their stronghold.

LANGUAGES

Common, gnollish, orcish, goblinese

Player's Name:	NPC	
Character's Name:	Olffgel Zookwar	
Race:	Gnome	
Class:	Mage	
Level:	7	
Alignment:	Neutral Evil	
THAC0:	19	

Height: 3'7   **Age:** 185

Weight: 82 lbs   **Sex:** M

Hair: ✕   **Eyes:** pink

HIT POINTS	ARMOR CLASS
19 / 19	10

ATTRIBUTES

	Attack Adj.	Damage Adj.	Weight Allow	Open Doors	BB/LG
STR 12	0	0	45	1-2	4%

	Reaction Adj.	Defense Adj.	Move Silently	Hide in shadows
DEX 14	0	0	✕	✕

	Hit Points Adj.	Shock Survival	Resurrection Survival
CON 10	0	70%	75%

	Languages	Learn Spell Chance	# of Spells Per Lvl
INT 16	+5	65%	11

	Magic Attack Adj.	Spell Bonus	Chance of Spell Failure
WIS 13	0	1st	✕

	Max # henchmen	Loyalty Base	Reaction Adj.
CHA 11	4	normal	normal

	current xp	xp for next lvl
Experience Points:	100,00	135,000

SKILLS

Gnome skills (+2 on saving throws vs wands and spells, infravision 60'), Wizard spells 1st: enlarge, sleep, charm person, spider climb, unseen servant, 2nd: invisibility, magic mouth, mirror image, web, wizard lock, 3rd: clairvoyance, feign death, haste, hold person, summon monster, 4th: polymorth other, 5th: animate dead

EQUIPMENT

Speedos, cape

GP: 125

HISTORY

This guy is a fucking pervert.

LANGUAGES

Common, gnomish, gnoll, goblinese, orcish, elven

Player's Name:	NPC
Character's Name:	Itaa Tohiish
Race:	Goblin
Class:	Ranger
Level:	2
Alignment:	True Neutral
THAC0:	19

Height: 3'2 **Age:** 22

Weight: 65 lbs **Sex:** F

Hair: ×   **Eyes:** yellow

HIT POINTS	ARMOR CLASS
14 / 14	7

ATTRIBUTES

STR 12	Attack Adj. 0	Damage Adj. 0	Weight Allow 45	Open Doors 1-2	BB/LG 4%
DEX 15	Reaction Adj. 0	Defense Adj. -1	Move Silently ✗	Hide in shadows ✗	
CON 10	Hit Points Adj. 0	Shock Survival 70%		Resurrection Survival 75%	
INT 5	Languages 0	Learn Spell Chance ✗		# of Spells Per Lvl ✗	
WIS 7	Magic Attack Adj. -1	Spell Bonus ✗		Chance of Spell Failure ✗	
CHA 11	Max # henchmen 4	Loyalty Base normal		Reaction Adj. normal	

Experience Points:	current xp	xp for next lvl
	3,200 /	4,500

SKILLS

Goblin skills: infravision 60', 50% resistance to disease, 20% move silently, 30% hide in shadows.

EQUIPMENT

Leather Armor, short bow (1d6), quiver of 20 arrows

GP: o

HISTORY

Itaa was born in the dungeons beneath Tardis Keep. She was one of the first females of her tribe to survive the warrior's rite of passage due to her skills with a bow. She was often treated as an outsider due to her independent personality and the fact that she was one of the most intelligent goblins in her tribe (even though she has an INT score of only 5). When most of her clan was killed by gnolls, including Yurtin, her mate-to-be, Itaa was brought into a life of slavery.

LANGUAGES

goblinese

maps

BAKERTON

tardis keep

ENTRY LEVEL

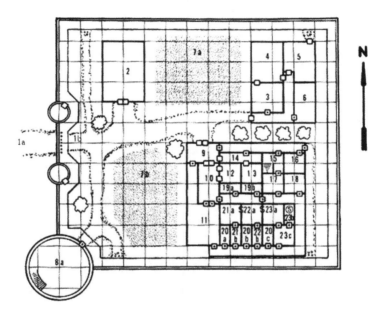

DUNGEON LEVEL

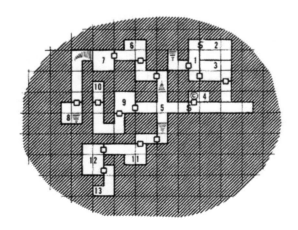

ancient
catacombs

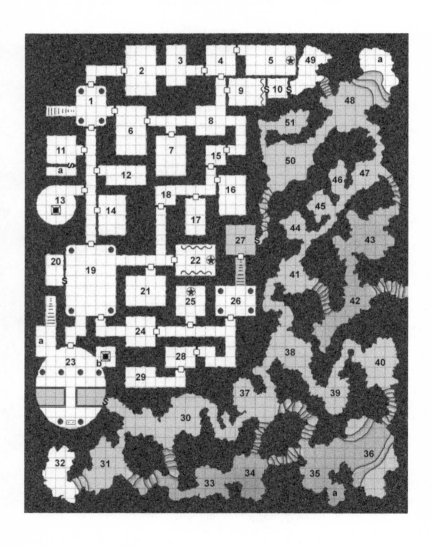

types of dice

d4   d6   d8

d12   d20   d10

MAGICAL ARTIFACT:
The Dildo of Enlightenment +2

INT: 11
EGO: 23
AL: Chaotic Good
VALUE: 17,500 gp

BACKSTORY

I really wish I never used the Dildo of Enlightenment +2. It happened just last week, and since then my whole world has been flipped upside-down. Glimworm, the kobold wizard, told us that the dildo possessed forbidden knowledge of the universe and that it should never be used under any circumstance. We agreed that we would not use the dildo. We would just retrieve it from the bandits who had stolen it from him, return it, then collect our reward and experience points.

The kobold wizard said, "You won't be tempted to stick it in your butts, will you?"

"No," I said, tapping the handle of my short sword +1. "We just want the reward."

"Are you sure?" repeated the kobold. "You're really not in the least bit curious about the forbidden knowledge locked away in the dildo?" Then he took a bite of a carrion crawler head on a long copper fork.

"Trust us," said Delvok, the elven ranger/cleric/mage/fighter, shaking his head. "We have no intention of sticking that ancient mystical relic in our rectums. No knowledge is worth that."

Glimworm sucked a tentacle into his reptilian dog-like snout and grunted.

"Good," he said. "Because if you were to use it then I'd have to kill you."

We nodded at him.

"I'm serious," he said. "If you use it I'll know. Then I will kill you."

I looked up at my two companions with a worried

expression. Delvok was equally worried, though he tried not to show it. But my other companion, a dwarf named The Dwarf Lord, had no idea what was going on. He never had any idea what was going on.

"We won't use it," I said. "Promise."

Glimworm slurped yellow goop out of the giant insect's head and then patted his scaled belly.

"Just remember . . ." he said.

Then he launched a magic missile at the wall behind us to demonstrate how serious he was. It made all of us jump, except for The Dwarf Lord, who leaned against his battle axe stroking his long red beard, thinking about something else.

We had planned to keep our promise to Glimworm. We really did. But then we were ambushed by two naked sex-crazed she-trolls who anally raped us with several items from my Bag of Holding: a mace handle, an iron holy symbol, some wolfsbane, a scroll of **Read Magic**, and the Dildo of Enlightenment +2.

The one that attacked me was the younger sister and less bulgy of the two. She wrapped her rubbery green body around me and wrestled me to the ground. Because her strength score was 7 points higher than mine and the fact that she was three times my size—I'm just a halfling, after all—she was able to hold me down and penetrate me repeatedly with a variety of objects until I was knocked unconscious.

When I came to, I found myself naked in the middle of the forest, all of my gold and food had been stolen, and the Dildo of Enlightenment +2 was sticking out of my anal cavity. Delvok was sitting under a tree, paralyzed with shock and unable to speak. Macra, an NPC, was lying dead face down in the mud, raped to death by the larger she-troll. It wasn't until I removed the dildo and put my chainmail back on that I became enlightened to the secret of my existence.

The knowledge I learned was that I am not actually a real being. I am nothing more than an imaginary character living inside of a Dungeons and Dragons tabletop RPG game. I do not have freewill of my own, because in another world there exists some shrimpy 14-year-old nerd named Mark Meador who controls me. My entire world is just a game to him, and I am just the character he plays in this game.

Delvok, who had also been raped with the dildo, learned that he is being played by a scrawny Trekkie kid named Buzz Jepson, who doesn't seem to know the difference between elves and Vulcans. And we learned that the Dungeon Master, the god who created our universe, is named Aaron Donnelly, the morbidly obese wheelchair-bound king dweeb of the school.

These wretched nerds are the gods of our world, and the worst part of it is they aren't really all that good at playing Dungeons and Dragons. The majority of them lack any sense of imagination, the Dungeon Master has only skimmed the DM rulebook, and they spend most of their time trading pewter figures or arguing over whose dice set they would use that day.

After obtaining this knowledge from the Dildo of Enlightenment +2, Delvok and I realized that we were completely fucked.

baKeRton

1: Bakerton Market

I meet up with Delvok in the market. He is wearing a dirty brown peasant's cloak, hiding his face. I didn't even recognize him until he waved me over.

"Polo," he says in a whispering tone, near the armory. "Come."

I look around and go to him.

"Why are you not cloaked?" the elf says, speaking in his usual Vulcan-like monotone voice.

"I didn't—"

"Were you followed?"

I shrug at him. "I'm a halfling. People hardly notice me."

Delvok nods, his eyes darting around the plaza to make sure nobody is paying attention.

Ever since we used the Dildo of Enlightenment +2, we have been in hiding. The kobold wizard is surely after us. We want to return the dildo and collect our reward, but Glimworm said he would know if we used the dildo and would kill us if

we did, so we can't just give it back to him. We are hoping that the wizard assumes that we were killed during our mission and the thieves got away with the magic item. We are hoping that we can just disappear and Glimworm will give up his search for the dildo. All we have to do is not be recognized by anyone in the area.

Neither Delvok nor I believe it will be that simple. Glimworm is a 9th level magic-user, after all, and he probably already knows that we have used the dildo. He has probably already sent out another party of adventurers to track us down and kill us, or he will come after us himself and cast Fireball all over our asses. Either way, we plan to keep a low profile for a very long time.

"It would have been very useful if we had a **Change Self** scroll at this time," Delvok says.

I agree and then ask, "Where's Dwarfy?"

"Trying to find us another quest. We need some gold pieces as soon as possible. Then we need to get out of this region and never come back."

"What kind of gig?" I go through my Bag of Holding, checking to see if I have any extra rations. "Something easy I hope."

"I told him to get us something outside of town, preferably a quest for characters levels 1-2."

"I doubt the Dungeon Master is going to allow us to go on a quest that easy," I tell him. "I'm level 3 now. Dwarfy is level 4. It's more likely that we'll go on a quest for characters levels 2-5."

"This would not be preferable," Delvok says, "for I am still only level 1."

"Yeah, because your idiot player wanted to be multi-class. I mean, according to the player's handbook, I don't think you're even allowed to be a ranger/cleric/mage/fighter. You can be a ranger/cleric or a cleric/mage/fighter, but all four? That's retarded."

"Yes, I agree that it is illogical." Delvok shakes his head. "I am not improving my skills by splitting up my experience points between four different classes. It would have been more logical to have chosen just one."

Then we notice that a blacksmith at the armory next to us has been listening to our conversation while hammering dents out of a full-plate helm. Delvok recognizes the eavesdropper giving us a confused stare, and motions for me to follow him. We step away from the armory and disappear into the crowd.

"We are to meet The Dwarf Lord at Orc Fall Tavern," says Delvok. "We shall head in that direction."

I nod at him and we dart through the crowd of peasants toward the tavern at the end of the road.

DM NOTE: BAKERTON RUMOR TABLE
[ROLL D00]

[1-7] There are a gang of gnolls raping and killing travelers to the east. (true)

[8-12] A halfling whore house is opening on the south side of town. (true)

[13-19] Glimworm, the master of the Mage Guild, was born a female gnome, but she uses Change Self to appear to be a male kobold. (false)

[20-26] A treasure of great value is hidden somewhere under Bakerton. (false)

[27-31] The master of the local Thieves Guild pays good money to adventures willing to perform live sex acts. (false)

[32-40] There are treasures hidden deep beneath the ruins of Tardis Keep. (true)

[41-54] There are two elf women looking for adventurers to accompany them into the ruins of Tardis Keep. (true)

[55-59] Hobgoblins are giving great blowjobs for only 5 gp just outside of town. (false)

[60-68] Bugbears have the best orgies. (true)

[69] Bisexual elf maidens will pay 10,000 gp for cunnilingus (false)

[70-98] Mark Meador is a total fag! (true)

[99-100] Do not trust the two elf women seeking adventurers. They have a long history of backstabbing their business partners. (true)

2: Orcfall Tavern

Orc Fall Tavern is crowded, as usual. This is the most popular drinking hole in the region for many adventurers, travelers, and assorted lowlifes. There are drunken barbarians pounding goblets on their tables as naked plump-bellied gnome women dance merrily for them on the counter top. There are a few rogues from the local Thieves Guild, plotting with whispery voices in the shadowy corner of the room. There are bards singing tales of heroic adventures. There are dwarven miners covered in soot.

If Glimworm has sent mercenaries to find us this would be the first place they would look, so we try to remain hidden. Delvok covers himself with his cloak and I hide behind his legs. We inch our way through the rowdy barbarians until we spot Dwarfy.

The Dwarf Lord is near the bar, raising his axe up and down to the rhythm of a bard song. The bard playing the tune for him is a blonde woman, who is very tall even for a human, standing like a stork over our stocky dwarf friend. She plays her lute with delicate pale fingers and sings about a magical forest filled with pixies and unicorns. As she sings, faeries fly around her head, dancing to the music with fluttering gossamer wings.

The Dwarf Lord nods his head at us as we sit down at the table next to him. We watch the faeries flying around the bard, wondering what the hell they are doing in here.

"I find this highly illogical," Delvok says, sitting in his chair with perfect Vulcan posture. "According to the Monster Manual edition 3.5, faerie folk, or the Fey, are elusive woodland creatures who prefer not to reveal themselves to humans, especially not in a common tavern."

"What do you expect?" I ask. "Our Dungeon Master sucks."

"Indeed," says Delvok. "My player should insist that he study the rulebooks more carefully."

We listen to the bard's song for a while, hoping that it will soon come to an end. Five rounds later, it is still going on.

Dwarfy points at the bard. "She's our new traveling companion!"

The human winks at us and continues to play.

"Another player character?" Delvok asks. "This bard?"

I examine the woman more carefully. Her leather armor is decorated with flowers and rainbows.

"Do you think it's Jenny?" I ask. "I bet you it's just Jenny."

Delvok nods. "That would be a likely assessment."

Jenny is our Dungeon Master's little sister. None of our players want her to play Dungeons and Dragons with them, because she always ruins the game. She's too young to really understand how to play RPGs and she always wants to be a faerie princess who rides a unicorn. She also wants to cast magic spells that don't really exist.

These are some examples of stupid spells she has made up:

Summon Pretty Unicorn (Conjuration/Summoning)

Level: 1	Components: V, S, M
Range: 0	Casting Time: 1 turn
Duration: permanent	Saving Throw: none

Explanation/Description: When this spell is cast a pretty unicorn appears with rainbow-colored hair and becomes my best friend forever and will save me whenever I'm in danger and can fly and talk and sing and dance and it's magical and can never die ever and only girls can cast this spell.

Speak with Mermaids (Alteration)

Level: 1   Components: V, S
Range: 0   Casting Time: 1 turn
Duration: permanent   Saving Throw: none

Explanation/Description: With this spell I can talk to a mermaid and then become best friends with her and I can ride on her back when she swims in the ocean and she'll take me to her underwater kingdom to have a mermaid ballerina ball where I'll marry a handsome prince who also is at the ball but not a merman because he lives in a big castle and is a brave knight too.

Create Magical Tea Party (Alteration)

Level: 1   Components: V, S, M
Range: 0   Casting Time: 1 turn
Duration: 15 turns   Saving Throw: none

Explanation/Description: This spell makes a magic tea party appear with delicious strawberry tea and pink cupcakes and fairies and talking animals that are invited to the tea party and sing and have cute outfits and hats too.

Rainbow Blast (Evocation)

Level: 1   Components: V, S, M
Range: 0   Casting Time: 1 turn
Duration: instantaneous   Saving Throw: none

Explanation/Description: A magical rainbow shoots out of my heart and causes all good people to be really happy and fully healed and at the same time kills all evil monsters in one second no matter how big they are.

Cure Lonliness (Abjuration)

Level: 1   Components: V, S, M
Range: 0   Casting Time: 1 turn
Duration: permanent   Saving Throw: none

Explanation/Description: This spell makes everyone become my best friend and they'll never call me names or make fun of me ever again no matter what even when I'm wearing my glasses and they will come to my house after school and play with me on the playground at recess always.

Aaron's mother always forces him to let his little sister play Dungeons and Dragons with him and his friends. If he doesn't let her play she throws a temper tantrum. The mother, not wanting to be disturbed while reading the latest selection from Oprah's book club, just lets the girl have her way. Jenny is the louder whiner of the two. It's just easier to let the more troublesome one do what she wants.

When the bard's song is finished, the woman introduces herself.

"My name is Robyn Woodsong," the bard says in a Cinderella voice. "I play pretty music for all the happy woodland creatures."

It is definitely Jenny playing this character. She has been magic-users, elves, druids, and even a mermaid with angel wings in the past. Now she is a bard. Aaron most likely explained the bard class as a type of magical singer. Since Jenny has recently gotten into the school choir, I bet she really liked the idea of playing a bard. She probably even wrote songs for her character to sing.

Writing and singing songs is the type of thing Jenny thinks is fun about playing Dungeons and Dragons, not going on quests and killing monsters. That's probably why the bard's song went on for so many rounds. She would have thrown a tantrum if she didn't get to sing the entire thing.

Jenny's characters are always the same: annoying and useless. It's a good thing they never last very long.

Robyn Woodsong sits down at our table next to me, but I don't say anything to her. My player purposely has me ignore her so that she will get bored with playing D&D and go do something else.

"This minstrel has brought news of a grand quest!" Dwarfy says, slamming his axe handle into the table.

Then he grabs a faerie out of the air and bites its head off, causing a thin fountain of blood to splash down his beard. He spits the head out into the bard's long golden hair.

Dwarfy continues, "Two elf wenches are looking for sturdy warriors such as ourselves to help them loot a nearby ruins!"

Robyn Woodsong cries as she pulls the faerie head out of her locks of hair. We ignore her whining.

"Let us go speak to them!" Then The Dwarf Lord smashes the table in half with his axe.

Todd Donnelly, who plays The Dwarf Lord, is Aaron's hyperactive 12 year old brother. When he plays Dungeons and Dragons in real life, he usually acts out every single thing his character does. Just now, when The Dwarf Lord smashed the table in half, Todd had karate chopped the table as hard as he could with his whole arm, causing pewter figures and twenty-sided dice to fly onto the floor. He even made the sound effect for the table breaking apart, with his lips pursed, spraying spit all over the maps and character sheets.

Then the dwarf raised his battle axe over his head. "Goblins beware! You are about to taste the steel of The Dwaaaaaaaaaaaaarf Loooooooooooooord!"

This is his catch phrase. He says it whenever he starts a battle, no matter what kind of monster he is fighting, and he doesn't care that it wastes a whole round in order to say it.

The Dwarf Lord leads us upstairs to a table with two elf women. One looks to be some kind of rogue and the other is some kind of magic-user.

The elf women seem very out of place for being in the world of Dungeons and Dragons. For starters, they both have enormous breasts. Elves aren't supposed to have enormous breasts. They are supposed to be thin, petite creatures. These elves are curvy, voluptuous women with full lips and hourglass figures. Their fashion style is also out of place and belongs only in the real world, not the Dungeons and Dragons world.

One of the elf girls is dressed like a punk rock chick. She has a green mohawk, green lipstick, many facial piercings, fishnet sleeves, a padlock chain necklace, combat boots, and blue jeans held up by a Bullet Belt of Protection +3. I can let the blue jeans and combat boots and even the mohawk slide, but why the hell does she have a bullet belt? There aren't guns in Dungeons and Dragons, let alone bullets. Yet, she is still wearing one because our jackass DM just doesn't give a shit.

The other elf girl has the style of a cyber goth. She wears black latex, aviator-style goggles, and 7-inch platform boots. She has purple makeup and purple dread falls in her hair, and for some reason that makes no sense to me at all she has a twelve-sided die tattooed on her lower back. Why the hell would a character in the Dungeons and Dragons universe get a tattoo of a twelve-sided die? Our players are fucking retarded.

The elf women are NPCs, or non player characters. I have learned that most of the people in my world are non player characters. This means the Dungeon Master controls them. Every adventure we ever go on we always get saddled up with a couple NPCs like these women, and usually they are very slutty characters who want to have sex with every single thing that moves. Although slutty elf women are nothing new to me, there have never been any punk or cyber goth girls in our world until now. I'm pretty sure they are here because my player, Mark, is really into the Suicide Girls website, which is loaded with pictures of naked punks and goths.

"I'm Juzii Alon," says the cyber goth in a thick Japanese accent. Don't ask me why an elf would have a Japanese accent. This one just does. She points to her punk friend and says, "This is Loxi Toa."

Loxi, the punk elf, sneers at me with her puffy green lips. That's when I realize she is topless. Why an adventurer would go on quests topless is completely beyond me. Our players would rather drool over the idea of adventuring with half-naked elves than actually giving them armor that might keep them alive longer.

The punk elf gives me a seductive look, then a wicked grin. "Hey halfling, you're kind of cute. Why don't you come and sit on my lap?"

I take a step forward, then hesitate. I can sense my player wants me to sit on her lap, but I try my best to resist him. "No, thanks."

The other characters sit down at the table next to the elves, taking up all of the available chairs.

"Looks like there's no place else for you to sit," Loxi tells me, grabbing me by the arm. "You have no choice but to use my lap as your seat."

The DM does a successful strength roll on the elf, so she is able to lift me up and place me in her lap like a puppy. She leans her body against my back so that her breasts are squished against the sides of my face. Just one of her breasts is bigger than my whole head.

"I've never had sex with a halfling before," she says. "If I fucked you I bet it would feel like I was molesting a child!"

You know, this is the kind of thing that really annoys me about living in a world that is controlled by horny 14-year-old virgins. These elf women are not real women. They are the women that these immature kids fantasize about. And sometimes I get the feeling that the only reason they play Dungeons and Dragons is so they can act out their sexual fantasies with each other. I'm not sure if these kids realize how pathetic (not to mention kind of homoerotic) this is.

I try to ignore the punk elf girl as she rubs her breasts against my head. It's good that Jenny's character is with us now. The Dungeon Master never gets us into any real graphic sexual situations while his little sister is around. He knows she would tell on him and then he might not be allowed to play Dungeons and Dragons anymore.

"So, we need some partners to help us on a quest," says Juzii, the Japanese cyber goth elf. "Have you ever heard of Tardis Keep?"

We shake our heads. I forget my head is between two breasts and my ears rub against them as my head shakes, causing Loxi to giggle flirtatiously.

"It was once a hidden fortress owned by Lord Tennant, a ruler who preferred to live an isolated life with his powerful army and seven wives. On the day he died, the fortress was abandoned and it fell into ruins. What we have recently discovered is that underneath the keep is a secret dungeon with a long forgotten treasure chamber that has yet to be looted."

Delvok nods his head. "This indeed sounds to be a profitable venture. Is there any proof to these rumors?"

"No," Juzii says, "but it's worth checking out, don't you think?"

"There's only one problem," Loxi says, her voice vibrating through her ribs against the back of my head. "Recently, a group of gnolls have taken over the ruins. We'll have to defeat the Gnoll King if we want to gain access to the dungeon.

That's where you come in."

"Yeah," Juzii says. "We can't defeat the gnoll gang all by ourselves, so we want to partner up with you lot. We can split all the gold we find six ways."

Then Loxi chuckles. "Unless some of you don't make it back alive. In that case, we'll have a more profitable split."

"So how does that sound?" Juzii says. "Are you in?"

All the player characters nod, except for Dwarfy who slams his fist into the table and says, "Let us slay this Gnoll King with our swords of justice! Let us not waste another moment and leave right away! Me steel be hungering for goblin blood!"

Then he raises his axe over the table, as if he wants us all to touch weapons in a kind of warrior's pact. None of us draw our swords, but Dwarfy continues in his pose for a few more rounds.

"What's a gnoll?" asks Robyn Woodsong.

Everyone groans and rolls their eyes. Our Dungeon Master really hates when his little sister asks questions like this in the middle of the game.

"It's like some kind of gnome troll I think!" Dwarfy says, his axe still dangling over the table.

"Oh," she says. "Are they cute? I don't want to slay them if they're cute."

"Silence, wench!" says The Dwarf Lord. "We are wasting time here! Let us journey to Tardis Keep and do battle with these gnoll scum! Then I'll shove an owlbear's severed head up the Gnoll King's ugly arse!"

Then The Dwarf Lord tries to cut the table in half, as he did the last one, but his attack roll fails. He tries again and rolls a 1 on the d20, a critical miss, which means he stumbles and loses a round. Not willing to give up, he continues his attempts to chop the table in half and continues to roll failing hits, even though the table's armor class is pretty low.

The rest of us grow bored with watching Dwarfy and leave Orc Fall Tavern to wait for him outside.

3: Old Mill Road

Without money to better equip ourselves, we decide to embark on our journey with what we've got. We take Old Mill Road out of town into the abandoned farm fields. This is an area we explored on our first mission—when I was level 1 with no experience points yet—which was a quest to track down a wereweasel that had been killing the farmers' livestock in the area. It was kind of a dumb mission, especially because the Dungeon Master thought it would be funny to have me get butt-fucked by a half-orc druid/thief.

The two elf women lead the way. Delvok and I stay back to talk amongst ourselves. As we walk, I can't take my eyes off of the punk elf girl's round ass showing prominently in her tight blue jeans. I'm probably staring at her ass because the Dungeon Master back in the real world is explaining to our players what these elf girls' asses look like in great detail.

Our Dungeon Master is often fixated on describing boobs

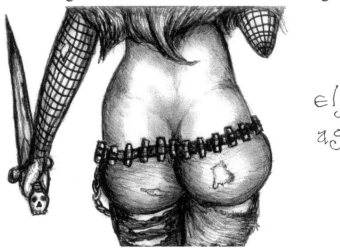

elf
ass

57

and asses, yet fails to explain in much detail the characteristics of the world around us. Like now, he really hasn't described what the farmland around us looks like. There's basically some fields and some farms I guess. I'm not sure what is actually in the fields. I don't even know what the weather is like, to tell you the truth. But the elf asses, I know exactly what they look like. They are vividly detailed.

Delvok notices that I'm ogling Loxi's rear end and says to me, "You might want to be careful of that one. She is a level 4 assassin of neutral evil alignment."

"How do you know that?" I ask.

"My player took a peek at her character sheet while the Dungeon Master was going to the bathroom."

"Oh," I say.

"So it is logical to assume that she plans to betray us at the end of the mission and steal all of our gold."

"We'll have to watch out then," I say.

"Indeed," Delvok says. "Being a level 1 ranger/cleric/mage/ fighter, I am no match for a level 4 assassin. It will be up to you and The Dwarf Lord to dispatch her if she turns on us."

"I'm no match for her," I say. "I'm just a halfling."

"But you are also a fighter," Delvok says.

"But I'm a fucking halfling fighter," I say. "There's nothing worse than being a halfling fighter."

"Why is this?" Delvok says. "I would find it more preferable than being a ranger/cleric/mage/fighter."

"No, it's much worse. Did you know that halflings can only get up to level 6 as a fighter? No matter how many experience points I get after level 6 I'll never be able to advance to level 7."

"Hmmm..." Delvok takes a long pause to think, rubbing his elven chin. "Yes, I see your problem. But, if I am not mistaken, you do have the option to dual-class at level 6. Do you not?"

"Not really. Halflings can only be fighters or thieves, but

my dexterity score is so low that I don't meet the minimum requirements to become a thief. I can only be a fighter."

"I see," Delvok pauses and lowers his head. "Your attributes do not work to your advantage. I doubt you will be able to survive any missions with myself and The Dwarf Lord once we have surpassed the sixth level."

I nod solemnly.

After giving it some thought, I decide not to let my level restriction ruin my spirits.

"I should look on the bright side, though," I say. "Since it'll take you four times longer than I to reach level 6, we can still go on adventures together for quite a long time. And perhaps maybe my player, Mark, will retire me after level 6. Maybe I'll be able to live the rest of my life in peace somewhere nice."

"That would be desirable," Delvok says. "But there is a good chance your player will just kill you off after you reach level 6. It is likely that our players would have more fun killing you than retiring you."

I shake my head. "I don't think Mark's like that."

Delvok raises his eyebrows, as if he knows I'm kidding myself.

"Well, the Dungeon Master doesn't really know what he's doing," I say. "Maybe he doesn't care if I'm allowed to go past level six."

"I do not believe that will be the case."

"Maybe Mark will beg him to let this rule slide."

"I do not think my player would allow the Dungeon Master to let even the smallest of rules slide."

Delvok's player, Buzz Jepson, isn't actually a big fan of

playing Dungeons and Dragons. He is more a fan of Star Trek. The only reason he plays D&D is because all of his friends are obsessed with it and because he thinks elves are the fantasy equivalent of Vulcans. He doesn't really care what elves are supposed to be like in D&D. He just pretends they are magical Vulcans. He even decided to name his character after an actual Vulcan from the Star Trek universe. Delvok is a great Vulcan composer mentioned in Star Trek: Deep Space Nine, whose music was appreciated by the Trill science officer Jadzia Dax.

Buzz doesn't just pretend he is a Vulcan when he plays Dungeons and Dragons. He pretends he is a Vulcan in his everyday life. At school, he walks down the hallway with his posture perfectly straight, his hair neatly parted, his eyebrows slicked up, his facial expression completely free of emotion. Although he's no longer allowed to wear a Star Fleet uniform to school, he still wears a tight-fitting pale blue shirt tucked into his pants and pretends it is his science officer uniform.

Although he tries to come off as a brilliant knowledgeable Vulcan like Spock, he actually is not very intelligent at all. Most of his grades are Cs and Ds. He has a learning disability and virtually no common sense. However, he still tries to come off as an intellectual to his peers, almost snobbishly so. He speaks with smart-sounding words, even though he has no idea what most of them mean. He often goes to the library and checks out large amounts of books on science and technology. Not so that he can read them, but so that he can carry them around school hoping to convince other people that he is reading them. Each week, he checks out a new stack of books. He has yet to read any of them.

At lunchtime, he plays chess in the library with the other unpopular kids who have nothing better to do during their break. He sits at a table, his back straight, his hands neatly folded, examining the chess board with a very serious face. When it is his move, he focuses more on his serious facial expression than his actual strategy.

Whenever he finishes making a move, he looks at his opponent and raises an eyebrow, as if expecting his opponent to be astonished by his brilliant play.

Whenever his opponent makes a move, Buzz curls his eyebrows downward and says, "I find that move highly illogical."

Whether the move is a logical one or not, Buzz has no idea. He just likes to say that. Most of the time, he loses a knight or his queen immediately after accusing his opponent of making an illogical move. This usually wipes the smug Vulcan look off of his face. Even though he has never won a chess game in his life, Buzz plays it every day at lunch time. Not just because his other friends have a different lunch hour than he does, but because he wants everyone to know that he prefers to spend his time on more intellectual activities.

Delvok looks at me and says, "It has been several hours since we have left town. I believe we should have hit a random encounter by now."

I look ahead and see the two elf girls are caressing each other's hips and grabbing each other's asses as they walk.

"Yeah, but our Dungeon Master is too focused on what those elves are doing right now," I say. "He's probably skipping random encounters."

Delvok nods his head. "Yes, he often skips them. I find it highly improbable that we would not at least be ambushed once by a gang of bugbears on our voyage to the keep. This region is crawling with bugbear patrols."

In the distance, we hear the sound of a twenty-side die rolling across a table. I stop in my tracks.

"Crap," I say. "Don't move. The DM just rolled for something."

"Could it be a random encounter?" Delvok asks, continuing down the path.

Then Delvok trips over a branch in the road and lands face first in the dirt. Then I hear the sound of a D4 as it rolls across the table. (Well, D4s don't actually roll, they kind of just plop down).

Delvok stands, holding a bloody nose. "It appears that I have lost a hit point."

"Already?" I ask. "But that's not fair. You're level 1. You hardly have many hit points to begin with."

"I am now down to only 5 hit points," he says. "It is a good thing I have a Cure Light Wounds spell ready. I might need to use it sooner than expected."

The others continue down the path, paying little attention to Delvok's minor injury. The Dwarf Lord attacks a scarecrow on the side of the road. His player rolls a critical hit and the scarecrow explodes with straw.

I shake my head at him and turn to Delvok. "Do you think Dwarfy is gaining any experience points by attacking those inanimate objects all the time?"

"I do not believe so," Delvok says. "But, since our Dungeon Master is an incompetent one he might decide to reward his brother a small sum of experience points for going through the effort."

"Maybe you should try it," I say.

"Thoughtlessly attacking every object in sight is not the appropriate behavior of a Vulcan," Delvok says. "I mean, an elf."

I laugh when he accidentally calls himself a Vulcan. He does this regularly, ever since I met him. Before I used the Dildo of Enlightenment +2, I always assumed when he called himself a Vulcan he was referring to a clan of elves that I was unaware of. Now that I know what Vulcans really are it is actually kind of funny.

specialty clothing shop inventory

CHAINMAIL FANNYPACK +1
This stylish fannypack is not only a convenient way to store gold pieces but also gives its wearer a +1 bonus to his/her armor class. COST: 240 gp

PIERRE CARDIN SUNGLASSES OF CLAIRVOYANCE
They don't actually give its wearer the power of clairvoyance, but they sure look cool, don't they? COST: 98 gp

ELVEN PONCHO
Similar to an elven cloak, but it's a poncho. COST: 450 gp

TIGHTY WHITIES OF OGRE STRENGTH
Think you're too cool to wear tighty whities? Well, what about a pair that gives you ogre strength, bitch? COST: 850 gp

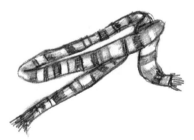

KLINGON WARRIOR COSTUME WITH HEADPIECE
Available in sizes for humans, Elves, Dwarves, and half-orcs. COST: 150 gp

DOCTOR WHO SCARF
Awards its wearer +5 nerd cred. COST: 25 gp

tardis keep

entry & level

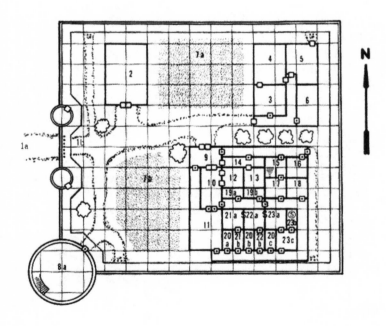

1a: Gates Exterior

We arrive at Tardis Keep before nightfall. The area is filled with rubble below ancient crumbling guard towers. The stone walls surrounding the keep are a shadowy gray, crawling with black thorny vines.

"This place seems ugly," says Robyn Woodsong. "I will use my magical song spells to turn this grimy castle into a peaceful pretty princess palace."

Then Robyn Woodsong plays her lute and casts **Grow Pretty Flowers Everywhere**. However, nothing happens, because that spell doesn't fucking exist. Being a 1st level bard, she doesn't have any spells to cast yet, let alone made up ones. Our Dungeon Master tells his little sister she can't do that and she tells him yes she can too or else she's telling Mom.

Then pink and purple flowers grow from all of the black vines along the walls of the keep. Our Dungeon Master tells his sister: "Fine, there, you happy now?"

Judging by the smile on Robyn Woodsong's face, I'm guessing that she is.

1b: Gates Interior

Inside the gates of Tardis Keep, we are greeted by a gnome NPC who is running through the courtyard toward us.

"Help!" cries the gnome, in gnomish tongue.

Luckily, I speak gnome.

"What is wrong?" I ask him in gnomish as he arrives to us.

He is covered in bloody wounds. Crouching down, he breathes rapidly.

"My family was captured by a group of gnolls," he says. "I escaped, but they still have my mother and sisters. You must help me—"

Then The Dwarf Lord says, "Ah-ha!!" and drives his battle axe through the gnome's head. "Taste my steel, you goblin scum!"

The gnome falls to the ground, dead. With only 2 hit points left and an armor class score of 10, he didn't stand a chance.

"What the fuck did you do that for?" I yell at the dwarf.

"I was getting bored!" Dwarfy says. "I finally got to kill something!"

"But he was friendly," I say. "He wanted our help."

"That was mean," says Robyn Woodsong. "You shouldn't be allowed to kill the good guys."

"Well, then he should have spoke in a language I could understand," says The Dwarf Lord. "Now, let's go find something else to kill!"

The Dwarf Lord runs off, all by himself, toward a barn near the north wall.

"This is not unusual behavior for our dwarf companion," Delvok tells me. "He is of chaotic neutral alignment, after all, so his actions are completely unpredictable."

"Yeah, but the gnome probably could have given us some information about this keep . . ."

"Perhaps," Delvok says, "but we will just have to get over this incident and move on. The gnome did say he had family members who were imprisoned by the gnolls. We might still be able to save them."

I nod my head in agreement.

"Now, we should go after him before he gets himself killed."

Our party agrees and we head in the direction of the barn.

2: Barn

We enter the damp, foul-smelling barn to discover The Dwarf Lord slaying a horse in one of the stables. The barn is filled with dead horses, some of which had been dispatched by our dwarf companion, others are dead from illness and malnourishment. The gnolls must not keep good care of their animals. Unless, that is, they were planning on using these horses for food instead of transport.

When Robyn Woodsong sees The Dwarf Lord killing the animals, she says, "Not the horsies!"

That doesn't stop the dwarf's rampage. Jenny begs the Dungeon Master to make him stop, but Aaron doesn't let her have her way this time. Their mother has finished reading her Oprah's Book Club book and is now at the store, picking up dinner.

The elf girls and I search the barn for valuables, but all we find are worm-infested horse blankets and blood-caked saddles. When the dwarf is finished messing around, we return to the courtyard.

7b: Gardens

Standing in the middle of a garden overgrown with weeds, which looks to have once been a decorative flowerbed, we try to decide where to go next. There is a tower in area 8 and a guardhouse in areas 3-6, but we decide to skip those and go straight for the main building. We know what these areas are because the DM has decided to openly show our players the map of Tardis Keep for a minute.

When our players decide to skip these areas, the Dungeon Master says, "Yeah, might as well skip them, there's not much in those areas anyway."

If I haven't stressed this enough already, Aaron Donnelly is a very lazy Dungeon Master.

9: Outer Hall

Upon entering the outer hall, Loxi says, "We need to find our way downstairs."

The room is empty. There are some broken mirrors and smashed chairs. Dozens of layers of brown footprints coat the floor from gnolls tracking mud in from the courtyard over the past few months. I bend down and examine the footprints. The prints came from some very large feet. They seem like they came from the feet of a large animal, not a humanoid.

"How large are gnolls again?" I ask Delvok.

Delvok says, "Judging by the foot size, I would estimate the height of these creatures is close to eight feet tall."

"Gnolls are that big? I always assumed gnolls were just gnome-sized trolls?"

Loxi enters the conversation. "Gnolls have nothing to do with gnomes or trolls. They are large humanoids with the characteristics of a hyena."

"Are they strong?" I ask.

"Pretty strong, yeah," she says.

Then she walks away, not really all that concerned. I decide to focus more on which direction we should take from here. Hopefully, there is a quick route downstairs that avoids most of the gnolls. There are four doors in this room that we can take, but two of them are locked.

"Which way should we go?" Juzii asks, her Japanese elf accent so thick we can hardly understand her.

I point at the ground. "Let's go in the direction with the least amount of footprints."

Everyone examines the ground, realizing that the biggest concentration of footprints lead from the front door to the double doors to the south. We rule out the double doors. The locked door next to the double doors also has a big concentration of footsteps. We decide to take one of the two doors to the east.

"Which one?" Loxi asks.

Juzii checks them for traps. "One of them is locked. The other is fine." She pulls out her thieves tools and attempts to unlock the door.

"You're a thief?" I ask. "I thought you were a magic-user?"

"I'm an illusionist/thief," she says, while trying to pick the lock.

"So we don't have a mage with us?" I ask. "Outside of Delvok?"

"I am able to cast illusionist spells," Juzii says.

Juzii's attempt to pick the lock fails. Before she has a chance to try again, The Dwarf Lord gets impatient.

"I'm sick of waiting around!" Dwarfy says, choosing the unlocked door. "Let's just take the easy route!"

He charges into the room. We reluctantly follow after him.

14: Guardpost

Within this room, an **orc (AC: 6, HD 1, hp 7, #AT 1, D 1-6)** is getting butt-fucked by a **bugbear (AC: 5. MV 9", HD 3+1, hp 20, #AT 1, D 2-8)**. When The Dwarf Lord realizes he is charging toward two dudes having sex, he comes to an instant halt, nearly tripping forward into the orc's large green boner which is aimed directly at the dwarf's waist-high forehead.

A little known fact is that all dwarves are incredibly homophobic. Because of this, dwarves will lose a round due to shock when witnessing naked humanoids of the same gender participating in homosexual acts. So Dwarfy must stand there, paralyzed in fear, as the bugbear gives it to the orc from behind.

Although the rest of us do not lose a round, we aren't quite sure what to do so we just keep our distance.

"Should we just leave them alone or something?" I ask.

"They aren't stopping," Loxi says, as she watches the humanoids thrusting and grunting.

"They're not allowed to do that!" says Robyn Woodsong. "That's gross!"

Back at the Donnelly home, Jenny tells her older brother she's going to tell their mom if he doesn't stop the orc and bugbear from having sex. But the Dungeon Master tells her that their mom is at the store and she can't do anything about it. The other players laugh at her.

When it goes back to being Dwarfy's turn, he raises his battle axe and releases his war cry: "Prepare to taste the steel of The Dwwwaaaaaarf Looooorrrd!"

Then the orc attacks the dwarf with his boner. He hits him in the right eye, causing him to lose a hit point. He will also be blind in that eye for one round. If the orc succeeded in ejaculating during his attack, then Dwarfy would have had an additional 1d4 rounds of blindness in that eye. The orc's ejaculation roll, however, failed.

Still not sure what to do in this situation, I decide to use my round to examine the room. It is an old guard post that has been transformed into storage. There seems to be nothing of much value in the room. The weapon racks are filled with rusty useless weapons. The barrels of grain are crawling with bugs. There are two doors in the middle of the room, but the two butt-fucking creatures are right between them.

"This is gross," Robyn Woodsong says. "I'm leaving."

Jenny has to go to the bathroom, so she has her character walk out of the room and wait in the Outer Hall. She tells her brother three times that he's not allowed to kill her while she's gone. He says he won't. She says he better not.

With his little sister out of the room, the Dungeon Master

A BUGBEAR BUTTFUCKING AN ORC

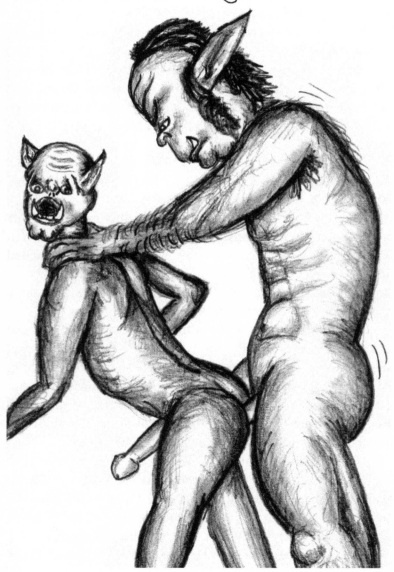

decides to make use of the NPCs. He has the two elf women make out with each other. He says they are getting turned on by watching the humanoids having sex and can't control themselves anymore. They pull down each other's pants and masturbate one another.

My player gets really into this. He really loves the idea of elf-girl-on-elf-girl action. He fantasizes about this kind of thing when he goes to bed almost every night. Although I can tell my player wants me to join in with the elves, I resist the temptation. Instead, he has me sniff the assassin's butt crack. I have no idea why.

"It smells like cranberry," the Dungeon Master tells my player.

My player has no idea why an elf ass would smell like cranberry, but he kind of likes it. He's an odd kid.

The Dwarf Lord is through with this sexual nonsense. He is here to kill and maim, and that's all. He attacks the orc's boner with his battle axe. His attack is successful and does 1d8 worth of damage, which rolls out to be a 7. The battle axe splits the boner in half and chops through the orc's midsection, killing him instantly.

The bugbear's penis goes in and out of the hole in the dead orc's stomach. After one round of attempting sex with the dead body, the bugbear loses his erection and becomes furious at the dwarf for robbing him of an orgasm. He grabs a rusted bastard sword from the weapon rack and releases a powerful roar.

"It appears that we have no choice but to kill this enraged Klingon," says Delvok, as he aims his longbow. Delvok often refers to bugbears and orcs as Klingons.

Delvok fires his longbow, but the arrow misses. Juzii and Loxi use their rounds to lick each other's breasts with their pierced tongues, which leaves me the only one left to attack.

I charge the bugbear with my short sword +1, but my player only rolls a 5. Big miss. The Dwarf Lord attacks successfully with his battle axe and takes off 6 of the creature's hit points.

"How do you like the taste of my steel!" cries The Dwarf Lord. "It tastes like Beef Stroganoff Hamburger Helper with blood and knives in it!"

The bugbear attacks and misses the dwarf. I attack and miss again. The Dwarf Lord lands his attack for another 8 points of damage.

"Have another!" cries The Dwarf Lord. "I stab you like I stab pumpkins with a screwdriver! I'll cut off your head with a garden hoe!"

The bugbear slashes at The Dwarf Lord with his bastard sword, causing 4 points of damage. I attack the bugbear and drive my short sword +1 through his belly, doing 5+1 points of damage. Nearly dead, the bugbear staggers on his feet.

Delvok sees this and decides to save his next arrow.

The Dwarf Lord says, "And I'll put your ugly wrinkled wart-covered penis in a pencil sharpener until it is nothing but shavings on the floor!"

The bugbear stabs Dwarfy while he continues his rant, taking off 7 points of damage.

"You're nothing but mud and dog poop to me! I crush you like a green army man half-melted in the microwave."

The Dwarf Lord then raises his battle axe for his ultimate finishing move, but his player rolls a 3 and he misses. Then it's my turn. On a roll of 18+1, I deliver the final blow, stabbing the bugbear in the side. Dead.

Although I saved The Dwarf Lord from losing any more hit points, he is not at all happy with me.

"Why'd you kill him?" he screams in my face. "He was my opponent! I was the one who was supposed to kill him!"

"Sorry," I say. "I thought you needed my help."

"You can help me if you want," says The Dwarf Lord. "But I am the one who delivers the finishing blows! I am the leader!"

"Fine," I say, although I have no idea why he thinks he's the leader.

"Remember that!" he says.

13: Study

We move on to the next room, through the unlocked door to the south. The two elves won't stop making out. Robyn Woodsong continues waiting in the Outer Hall. The Dwarf Lord is still incredibly pissed he didn't get to kill the bugbear. Because there are no creatures in this room to fight, the dwarf decides to attack the chairs and bookshelves of the study.

all elves are bi

Todd Donnelly, who plays The Dwarf Lord, is an incredibly awkward kid. He is two years younger than his brother, Mark, and Buzz, but his maturity level seems several years younger than that. He is so hyperactive that he's hard to really understand sometimes. His teachers put him into special education classes, not because he had a learning disability but because he is nearly impossible to keep under control. He constantly disrupts any class he is in, usually so that he can get laughs out of the other students. However, nobody really understands his jokes.

He'll say something like, "Look, the ceiling is pooping out banana men!" Then he would make a farting noise. "Look, that one came out as diarrhea!" Then he'd laugh really loudly at himself and elbow the kid next to him. "Banana diarrhea!" He has no idea that nobody thinks he's funny. They always think his rantings are annoying and immature, even for a 12-year-old.

Our players take a break from playing Dungeons and Dragons to eat dinner. Aaron's mom brought some fried chicken from the grocery store deli, with a side of coleslaw, potato wedges, and that crappy dessert that is just strawberry jello mixed with whipping cream. To drink, they have a choice between RC Cola and sugar-free Grape Shasta.

Todd Donnelly drinks Grape Shasta because he isn't allowed to have caffeine. Even without the caffeine, he is still speaking at the top of his lungs, sitting on the edge of his seat, and grinding his teeth between sentences. He's just naturally wired this way.

"Look at me!" Todd says as he puts chicken skin all over his face. "Look, I'm an orc!"

Even though they sit next to each other at the dining room table, my player ignores the kid. He really doesn't like Todd. Mark is a very shy, reserved person, so he finds the loud unrestrained behavior of this kid to be obnoxious and offensive. Buzz and Aaron also ignore him because they are busy arguing about which science-fiction television series is the superior one: Star Trek or Doctor Who.

Since the three of them are ignoring Todd, he turns his attention toward his little sister. He makes growling sounds as he reaches his arms out to his sister, coming in close to her with the chicken skin all over his face.

"Jenny!" Todd cries. "I'm an orc! I'm going to get you!"

Jenny says, "You're so gross!"

"I'm going to give you a kiss!" Todd says.

"Mom!" Jenny cries.

The mom is eating dinner in the living room with their father and their older college-aged brother, watching football. The mother ignores them. That's usually how she prefers to handle her kids.

Todd takes the chicken skin off of his face and throws it at his sister.

"Quit it!" Jenny cries, her chubby cheeks becoming red with frustration. "Todd, you're grounded!"

Even though she's only ten years old, Jenny is a bossy little kid. Their parents let her have her way so much that she thinks she can order her older brothers around. She will often tell them when they are grounded or in trouble. She makes sure that they are always following the rules.

"You can't ground me!" Todd says. "I'm an orc!"

He grabs her by the arm and pulls on it, knocking her drumstick out of her hand. When Jenny sees her dinner on the floor, she screams at the top of her lungs like a spider has just crawled into her underwear.

"Goddamnit!" The father puts his plate of food down, gets out of his lazy boy, and goes to the dinner table.

"Todd, leave your sister alone!" the father says, standing in the dining room entryway with his tight white shorts pulled up too high. "I don't want to hear one more word out of any of you!"

"But dad," Jenny says, "he threw my chicken on the floor! Then he stepped on it and spit on it!"

When telling on her brothers, Jenny always exaggerates so that they will get into more trouble. However, unlike their mother, their father doesn't give a shit.

"Just wash it off," says the dad. "It's fine."

Jenny looks at the chicken on the floor and pouts.

The dad looks at Aaron. "Keep your brother and sister under control. If I have to come in here on more time I'm taking your friends home and they won't be spending the night."

Aaron nods his head. When the dad leaves the room, Aaron makes an angry double-chin face to mock his dad. Everyone snickers quietly. It even cheers up Jenny, who always laughs when Aaron makes the double-chin face. Before they get into trouble again, they decide to sneak their food into Aaron's room, to continue playing Dungeons and Dragons while they finish eating.

"Where were we again?" Aaron asks.

None of them remember.

"Mark just killed my bugbear," Todd says.

"Okay, so you're in the study," Aaron says.

Jenny says, "I'm still in the first room because I didn't want to be around those naked pervert monsters."

"Okay, let's go back to her then," Todd says. "I want to get into a real battle now."

"If you want a real fight," my player says, "we should go through the double doors in the first room, the one where all the gnoll footprints lead."

"Yeah, let's go there!" Todd says.

"Okay," Aaron says. "You go through the double doors and arrive in a great dining hall . . ."

10: Dining Room

The dinner table in this room is large enough to accommodate twelve people. It is vacant at this time but seems to have been used in the recent past. We decide to eat some dinner at this table, gathering gnoll food from the kitchen in area 12. As we dine, our players pretend to be us in the real world, eating the rest of their food as if it were the food of the gnolls.

"Ahh!" says The Dwarf Lord, tossing the bone of his drumstick at the wall behind him. "That was a fine meal for a barbarian dwarf!"

In the real world, Aaron yells at his brother for throwing food into his laundry basket. Todd doesn't break character.

"But I'm a barbarian!" says the dwarf. "I don't clean up after myself." He turns to Robyn Woodsong. "Wench, clean it up for me!"

"No way!" says Robyn Woodsong.

Loxi gets up, flicks Dwarfy's ear as hard as she can, and retrieves the bone. The dwarf rubs his ear as she drops the bone back into his plate.

"So where should we go next?" I ask, having finished my food quite a while ago and am ready to move on.

Besides the two doors that lead into the kitchen, there are two doors out of this room. One to the east and double doors to the south.

"Let me check them for traps," Juzii says.

She checks the doors. Both of them are locked. She gets on her knees and uses her Open Locks skill. She is successful with both doors.

"I think we should split up!" says the dwarf. "I'll go in the southern doors with Delvok and Robyn! The rest of you can go through the other door!"

We look at each other.

"Splitting up would not be logical," Delvok says. "There is safety in numbers."

"Then all of you go one way and I'll go the other!" Dwarfy says. "I want to kill something on my own without anyone's help!"

"I think splitting up is a good idea," Loxi says, looking

down at me.

Juzii comes to me as well. "Yeah, we could use some time alone with the halfling."

"So that's three votes saying we should split up!" says the dwarf. "Who is the tie breaker?"

Loxi lifts my hand for me. "He votes we separate as well."

Before I could say, "No I don't," Juzii covers my mouth with her hand.

"It is decided!" says The Dwarf Lord. He points his battle axe at the doors to the south. "Onwards, to battle!" Then he charges through. Robyn and Delvok follow after.

"Looks like we got you to ourselves," Loxi says, pressing her bare breasts into my face.

"Don't worry, we'll take good care of you," Juzii says, licking her Asian elven lips.

19a-19b Servants' Rooms

I lead the elf women down a hallway and discover two rooms, both which are servant barracks. There are three **goblins (AC: 9, HD 1-1, hp 3, 2, 2, #AT 1, D 1-3)** in area 19b, which are servants to the Gnoll King and his men. The goblins are weak and old. They're not up for any kind of fight.

"Goblins?" Loxi says, drawing her swords. "Sorry, buddies, but you're not allowed to watch."

"Watch what?" I ask.

Loxi corners the sickly goblin men and hacks them down one at a time. Her tan naked breasts bounce up and down as her sword plunges into goblin skulls. They try to defend themselves, but their attacks can't touch her. They shriek and beg for mercy.

When there is only one of them left, I say, "Let me talk

to him. I speak goblin."

"They are scum," Juzii says, standing above me. "Let them die like scum."

Loxi cuts the throat of the final goblin and then wipes her blade and her breasts off on the cleanest bed sheet she can find.

"Now, let's get to it," Loxi says as she walks toward me.

"Get to what?" I say.

"Sex," Juzii says, kneeling down to pull off my chainmail.

Damn horny teenagers. They're already starting with the pervy bullshit. Why can't they just invent a porn RPG for these kids to play and leave me out of it.

I pull away from the elves. They both just laugh at me.

"You can't resist, tiny man," Loxi says. "We're almost twice as big as you."

I go for the door.

"No you don't," Loxi says. "Juzii, get him!"

Juzii waves her fingers and casts **Hypnotism** on me. My player fails the saving throw and I become under her control.

"Take off your clothes and submit to us," Juzii commands.

I am not able to deny this request while under her spell.

I slip out of my chainmail and underclothing. The elf girls giggle at the size of my penis.

"He *is* like a little boy," Juzii says.

"I know," Loxi says. "I like it. Sex with halflings is like a legal way to indulge my pedophilia fetish."

"You have a pedophilia fetish?" Juzii asks.

"I have every fetish," Loxi says.

Juzii laughs, then turns to me. "Then we should roleplay that he's a child we've abducted, and we're going to molest him."

"Good idea," Loxi says. "Let's tie him up before the spell wears off."

I agree to lie on a goblin bed as they tie my limbs to the bedposts.

"Hey little boy," Loxi says, rubbing her thin fingers down my chest to my penis. She stares up at me with her Asian eyes and blows on my penis until it becomes erect. Then she puts it in her mouth for a second and rolls it around on her tongue.

Then she says, "It's so small I could swallow it whole."

In the real world, I notice that it's just Mark and Aaron in the room. Since the others aren't playing in this section, they've decided to go play Lego Star Wars on the Nintendo WII. Mark feels kind of awkward roleplaying an erotic session with just the two of them in the room. He is not at all into the whole bondage/pedophilia thing.

But the Dungeon Master is doing this not for Mark's benefit, but for his own. Now that I'm tied down, there's not really anything Mark can do to participate in the game. He just has to sit back and let Aaron describe what his NPCs are doing.

Aaron has a fetish for Asian girls. He also likes the idea of being molested by older women. Juzii, the Japanese elf, was created by Aaron to resemble his 8th grade English teacher. She was a young teacher, in her mid-twenties, who was born in Japan. She also was kind of a cyber goth. Although she didn't look it anymore, she used to be a goth/rave girl when she was in college. She always talked about how she used to look as a way to relate to her students.

To say Aaron had a crush on his teacher would be an understatement. Every night, Aaron would fantasize about having sex with his teacher. He wanted her to seduce him to come home with her and then keep him in a cage. He wanted her to molest him every night and use him as her sex slave. This is why he has Juzii going after me, the halfling. It's like he's acting out his fantasies with his English teacher.

Juzii removes her latex clothes and crawls on top of me, her body blocking out all light. Her mass twice mine as she peers down at me with those dark hungry eyes. Then Loxi comes up behind her and gives her oral sex. Juzii shoves her breasts into my face and moans softly. Then she kisses me, her lips covering most of the lower half of my face.

Loxi grabs my penis between Juzii's legs and strokes it until it is erect again. Then Loxi pulls off her jeans and squats down on top of me, sliding my tiny penis into her enormous vagina.

Juzii turns around and presses her hairless vagina into my face. It is a known fact that elves do not have any body hair, not on their arms, legs, armpits, or pubic region. Halflings, however, tend to be attracted to body hair on women, especially pubic hair.

"If you cum too soon and lose your erection I'm going to stab you with a poisoned dagger," Loxi says to me. She fucks me with all of her weight crushing my midsection. Her thighs on each side of me are as big as my entire torso.

Juzii forces me to give her oral sex. She commands me to tickle her clit with my tiny tongue. For some reason, the Dungeon Master describes her pussy taste as similar to butterscotch and peaches. She whimpers as she reaches orgasm.

My player can tell the Dungeon Master is getting way too into all of this. It's getting a little too creepy for him. Mark knows all about the fantasies Aaron has had involving

halflings are easy to Rape

his 8th grade English teacher. Mark found the idea rather disturbing. Not because the teacher wasn't an attractive woman, but because Aaron is a zit-faced morbidly obese cripple who was perhaps the ugliest kid in the school. The idea of that woman keeping Aaron as a sex slave was an incredibly disgusting image. Even more disgusting to Mark is watching Aaron drool all over his maps and notes as he describes the actions of the two elf women.

When Juzii cums against my face, she grinds her massive weight into me, driving my head down onto the wooden goblin bed. I lose 2 hit points in the process.

Then it's Loxi's turn. She unties me and I find myself fucking her doggie-style, my chest bouncing against her globular butt cheeks. I can't really see anything past her wide fleshy mounds. Her ass is so big compared to me that I feel like my entire body might get sucked within.

As I have sex with the elf, my player rolls every round to see how successful my strikes are. He has to make rolls against my dexterity and strength to see how long I can last. The elf moans as she slams her ass against my body. Juzii kisses my neck and presses her breasts against my back.

Mark rolls a critical hit, causing me to succeed in giving Loxi a powerful orgasm. Then his ejaculation roll succeeds, just barely, as I cum inside of Loxi's deep cavernous meat tunnel.

Deep cavernous meat tunnel is the exact phrase the Dungeon Master used to describe Loxi's vagina.

When we are done, the elf girls pat me on the head like they would a puppy who had just performed a neat trick. Then we get back into our clothing.

As I put my chainmail back on, I notice the girls are staring at me, giggling.

"What?" I say.

They turn away from me and laugh at each other, then look back.

"What?" I say.

Loxi pulls up her jeans over her bald dripping vagina and buckles her Bullet Belt of Protection +3.

Then she says, "You just got Scrot Rot, bitch!"

Both girls laugh.

"Scrot Rot?" I ask.

"We gave you our STD," Juzii says.

Aaron explains to my player that many elves are carriers of the Scrot Rot disease, but it doesn't effect elvenkind. Only the people elves have sex with.

"What?" I say. "You think that's funny?"

They high-five each other.

I realize now that I have the Scrot Rot STD, I have a –2 adjustment to my constitution and –1 adjustment to my charisma.

"This is bullshit!" I say.

"Elf pussies will rot your balls off!" Loxi says.

They continue to tease me as we leave the room.

In the real world, Todd, Buzz, and Jenny are bored of waiting around and they want to play again. The Dungeon Master focuses on their quest now, and my player is forced to leave Aaron's bedroom for a while. He decides to play Left 4 Dead in Todd's room.

When they're ready for him, I am back in the game.

11: Throne Room

When I enter this chamber, I find The Dwarf Lord, Delvok, and Robyn Woodsong in the middle of a fight with **7 gnoll marauders (AC: 5, MV 9", HD 2, hp 15, 15, 14, 14, 14, 13, 13, #AT 1, D: halberds, 1-10)**. One marauder is already dead and two are wounded. Although this is the throne room, the Gnoll King is not present. These guards were protecting the king's throne from intruders when Dwarfy and the others stumbled into them.

The gnolls are even larger and more ferocious than I expected. They surround Dwarfy and Robin Woodsong, growling and barking at them in gnoll-tongue.

Delvok is in the back, firing arrows at the gnolls. Judging by all of the arrows sticking out of the walls and floor, he hasn't been too successful at hitting any of his opponents.

When Delvok sees the elf girls and I approaching him, he says, "I was correct in the assessment that splitting up the party was a bad idea. The Dwarf Lord is down to nearly half of his hit points and I am down to two."

"You should cast heal," I tell him.

"I am considering retreat before healing," Delvok says.

"Retreat sounds good," I say. "I don't see how we stand a chance otherwise. I mean, look at those gnolls. Avoiding them is far more preferable to fighting them. I think we should run away and come back later."

"I suggest we run away and do not come back later at all," Delvok says.

We back away, wondering if we should tell our companions to flee or leave them here so they can keep the gnolls occupied while we make our escape. I'm voting for the latter, probably because my player doesn't want to have to deal with Todd or Jenny anymore.

Robyn Woodsong is down to her last hit point, but doesn't realize how serious her situation is. Her player doesn't really know what hit points are for.

"Don't worry," Robyn says. "My magic will save us all!"

Then she casts **Turn All Monsters Into Happy Dancing Leprechauns That Want To Be Best Friends With Everyone**. Nothing happens, of course, because her player was just making up fake spells again. So Robyn Woodsong just waves her hands around, pretending to cast a spell. Then a gnoll chops her head off with the blade of his halberd polearm.

"Crap!" cries The Dwarf Lord. "We lost the bard! Her head's been cut clean off!"

In the real world, Jenny tells her older brother that he's not allowed to kill her character. He tells her it's too late, she's already dead. She runs out of the room and tells their dad Aaron killed her character and spit in her face and used bad language, but her dad tells her it's time to go to bed and that she should leave her brother alone.

"They're too much for you," I yell at The Dwarf Lord. "Let's just get out of here."

The Dwarf Lord chops a gnoll's leg off and then stomps on its chest as it hits the ground.

"Never!" Dwarfy says. "I'll kill them all!"

I shrug and turn to the others. "Escape?"

"Escape," they all say, nodding their heads.

The three of us run to the exit to the south. While Juzii picks the lock to the door, we watch The Dwarf Lord get hit with halberds from two different sides.

"Do you think he has a chance?" I ask Delvok.

"None at all," Delvok says.

Dwarfy slashes with his battle axe, attacking them one

at a time.

"Attack me all you want!" he yells at the gnolls. Then he staggers back as one of them hits him in the chest again. "But you will now all fall to the power and the might and the steel of The Dwaaaaaaaarf Loooooooord!"

Then the dwarf stretches out his arms and unleashes his special barbarian ability: the berserker rage. With the extra hit points and attack bonuses, he charges the gnolls, ready to take them on all by himself.

The rest of us decide not to wait around to see what's going to happen to him. We flee as soon as the dwarf uses his rage.

20a-c, 21b, 22b: Prison Cells

We come to a hallway lined with prison cells. As Delvok casts **Cure Light Wounds** to bring his hit points back up to 6, the rest of us examine the cells. Inside, there are gnomes, goblins, and orcs separated by race and gender. Juzii picks the locks to free the gnomes, but she decides to leave the orcs and goblins in their cells. The orcs become enraged by the elf woman for not letting them out.

"You can rot in there," Loxi tells them in orcish.

"Let me out so I can kill you!" yells the alpha orc. "I will rape your ugly elf cunt!"

Loxi laughs at him, grabs her tits, and points them at him like crossbows. "Just try it, limp dick."

The orc slams his head into the bars of his cage, trying to get out. His friends reach out at her, swinging fists in her direction. Loxi draws a broad sword and cuts one of their arms off and walks away.

Most of the goblins do not have the energy to complain.

They are defeated, worn down slaves of the gnolls. They no longer understand the meaning of freedom. All of them except for one goblin. It is a female goblin, staring at me through the bars. She has yellow eyes and green skin with black stripes tattooed across the sides of her arms and legs. The others are yellow-skinned with red eyes and circular tattoos. They must belong to separate clans. She just watches me as the gnomes are released and the other humanoids, including herself, are left to rot.

There are seven gnomes. Two adult females, two male children, and three female children.

"We are trying to get downstairs," Juzii tells the gnomes. "Have you seen the entrance to the dungeon?"

The gnomes shake their heads. Most of the children are in shock. Only one of the adult females is able to function. Many of them are covered in fresh blood. It appears that many of their friends and family were recently massacred in front of them.

"We need to get downstairs," Loxi says. "Can you help us or not?"

"We've only just arrived," says the female gnome.

"We can't take you with us," Juzii says. "If you're not going to be of any use to us you'll have to stay here. You'll only slow us down."

"You can't leave us," the gnome says.

"It would not be logical for you to accompany us," Delvok says in gnomish, with a Vulcan accent. "Where we are going will only put you into greater danger. If we succeed in our mission we will come back for you. However, it might be more prudent for you to attempt an escape on your own."

I consider telling them about the gnome we met at the gates of the keep, but decide that might not be the best thing for them to hear right now. Our dwarf companion did slaughter him mercilessly.

"But I don't know what to do without you," the gnome

says, then she begins to cry. "They're just children. Won't you help us free these children? You can continue your quest after they are safe."

Loxi points her sword at the gnome. "I'm helping you by not cutting your head off right now. That's about as much as you'll get out of me."

She turns to me. "You understand, don't you? You'll help us."

I shake my head. "I'm sticking with my group. If they refuse to help you then you're on your own."

She cries and buries her large nose into my chest.

"If you're too scared to escape on your own just wait here," I say. "We'll get you on the way back."

"Promise?" she asks.

"Yeah, I promise," I say.

Loxi laughs. "As long as he survives that long, that is."

21a: Food Storage

Juzii unlocks the door on the other side of the gnome's prison cell. We enter the room to discover barrels of water and crates of food. The water is brown and smells of rust. The food is rancid and maggoty. This is what the gnolls are feeding to their prisoners.

"The gnomes couldn't survive off of this," I say.

"Yeah," Loxi says. "But the orcs and goblins probably love it. They can live off of pretty much anything."

Juzii discovers a secret door on the east wall. She opens it and we follow her in.

22a: Equipment Storage

This is where the gnoll guards keep the personal belongings of their prisoners. There's some orc armor and weapons, but almost anything of value has already been claimed.

The southern wall of the room faces the goblin cage. The goblin girl is now on this side of her cell, staring at me through the bars. As Juzii searches for another secret door, the goblin waves me over to her.

"Pssst," says the goblin girl.

I go over to her.

"What?" I say in goblinese.

"Dungeon help?" whispers the goblin girl. "Itaa help you."

The others notice me talking to the goblin, but since none of them know the language they ignore us.

"How?" I say.

"Itaa know castle better anyone," she says. "Itaa show dungeon. Itaa know dungeon."

"Are you lying?" I ask.

"Itaa no lie," she says.

"Your name is Itaa?" I ask.

"Itaa Tohiish," she says.

I turn to the elf women. "This goblin says she can show us the way into the dungeon."

Juzii and Loxi look at each other, then approach the goblin.

"Ask her to tell us how to get there," Loxi says.

"They want you to tell us how to get there," I tell the goblin.

"Let Itaa out," she says. "Itaa tell."

"She wants us to let her out first," I say.

"Tell her that if she's lying I will cut her throat," Loxi says.

I tell her. Itaa's yellow eyes grow wide. "No lie, no lie," Itaa says. Then Juzii lets her out of the cage.

"We can't let your friends out," I tell her, gesturing to the other goblins.

"Friends?" Itaa says with an annoyed tone, looking down at the yellow goblins with disgust. "No friends. These worthless gaa'taat." Then she spits on them as the cage door closes them in. "Not Itaa clan."

Itaa goes straight for the boxes of equipment in the center of the room. She takes out a short bow and a quiver of arrows.

"No weapons," Loxi says.

The goblin stares with empty yellow eyes at her.

"I'll carry your weapons for now," I tell Itaa.

"Itaa good with arrow," Itaa says. "Itaa help with fight."

"Sorry," I tell her. "They don't trust you."

The goblin girl nods and hands me her weapon. I put it in my Bag of Holding.

"Good bow," says Itaa. "Take care."

I agree. Then we leave the room through a secret door on the east wall.

23a: Wolf Cage

The next room is filled with the bodies of six dead wolves. Judging by the state of their decay, they must have been killed only recently, within the past day or two. They don't even stink much yet. These wolves were most likely the pets and companions of the gnolls, before they were killed.

When the goblin girl sees the dead wolves, she snickers.

"What?" I say, as she laughs.

"Itaa kill wolves," she says. "Poison to dead."

She continues to laugh.

"You poisoned the gnolls' pets?" I ask.

"Yes," Itaa says, kicking one of them in the head. "Itaa hate gnolls. Itaa like kill wolves."

She slaps her little green knee and laughs louder.

"Would you mind calming her down?" Delvok asks. "We are next door to a guard station."

I tell Itaa to keep quiet. She nods at me.

"Itaa quiet," she says in a not-quiet voice.

23c: Guard Barracks

This is the guard post and barracks for the gnolls who keep watch on the prisoners. There are only two gnoll guards here, one sleeping in a chair, the other sleeping on a bunk so small that all of its hairy limbs are off the sides and draped across the floor.

"Shit," I whisper at Delvok. "More gnolls."

Delvok nods at me, then whispers, "I will handle this."

He waves his hands and casts **Sleep** on the sleeping gnolls. Then he raises his eyebrows at me, as if digging for compliments.

"What the fuck was that?" I ask Delvok in a near yelling voice.

"What?" Delvok says.

"They were already asleep!" I yell. "Why the fuck did you waste your only wizard spell to put two gnolls to sleep when they were already fucking asleep?"

Delvok tries to keep his calm. "We are not in a position to fight gnolls. It seemed logical to keep them asleep."

"Well, we could have at least tried to sneak past them first," I said. "If they happened to wake up then it would be the time to cast **Sleep** on them."

"I do not see your logic," Delvok says.

"That spell really could've come in handy later," I said. "You wasted it for nothing."

"It will only be wasted if we continue to debate this topic until the spell wears off," Delvok says. "I suggest we move on."

I shake my head, then turn to the goblin. "Which way?"

Itaa points to the north door.

"Itaa know shortcut," she says.

Juzii picks the lock and we enter.

23b: Closet

We squeeze into this tiny room and close the door. There aren't any doors or windows in this room.

"Now what?" I ask.

"Down," Itaa says, pointing at the floor.

She pulls back a rug to reveal a trapdoor leading to the dungeon below. It is a trash shoot, used by the Gnolls to dump pieces of dead prisoners. The hole is incredibly narrow, too small for most humanoid-sized creatures.

Itaa opens the door and sticks her legs in, ready to climb down.

"We can't fit through there," Juzii says.

"Yeah, that's too small of a space," Loxi says. "Even if I could get my ass through, I'd get stuck at my bust."

I grab the goblin before she drops down.

"Wait," I tell Itaa. "It's too small for the elves."

"Huh?" Itaa says, looking at the manhole and then the elves, then back and forth again, until she understands her mistake. "Oh. Boobelf no fit. Hrmm."

She puts her thin fingers against her round little chin. "There another way, but this way problem."

I tell the others about the alternate route that Itaa explains to me. The main stairs to the lower floors is in area 15 of the map. We can get to it through area 17. However, the door to area 17 is **Wizard Locked** from the outside. Since we don't have a **Knock** spell, the only way through would be to open the door to this area from the other side.

"Itaa go down this way and come up other side," Itaa says. "Itaa open door for you."

I tell the others her plan.

"You go with her," Loxi says.

"Me?" I ask.

"You're the only other person who can fit down there," Loxi says.

"It is logical that she would attempt an escape if she goes alone," Delvok says. "It would be prudent for you to accompany her on this quest."

Itaa agrees that I should go with her.

"Come with Itaa, Halfman," she says. "We two go."

She slides through the trap door. I look down at the darkness below and then look back at my companions.

"Hurry up," Loxi says. "She might prepare an ambush for you if you wait too long."

I take a deep breath and then slide down after her.

TYPES OF POLEARMS

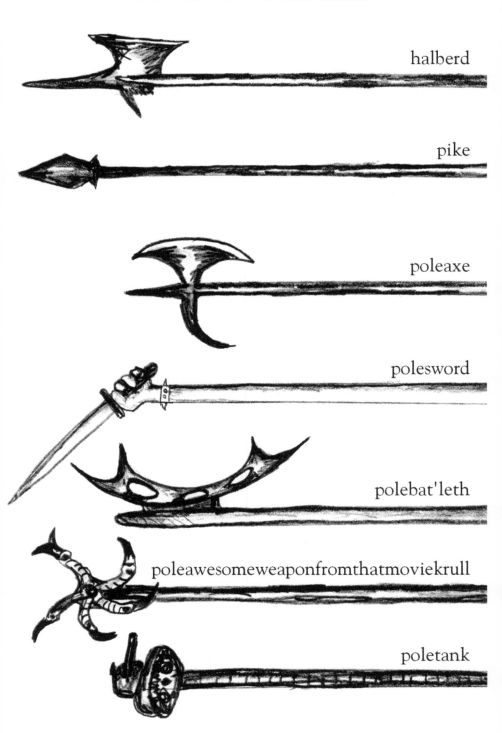

halberd

pike

poleaxe

polesword

polebat'leth

poleawesomeweaponfromthatmoviekrull

poletank

tardis keep

dungeon
level

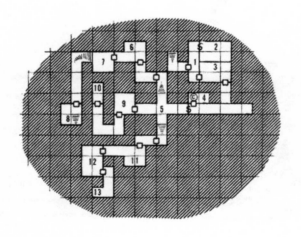

4: Garbage Pile

I land next to Itaa in a pile of bones and refuse. I was wrong about the gnolls throwing bodies of dead prisoners down this trash shoot. The gnolls must eat the dead prisoners first and then toss the scraps down here. The stench of rotten meat is thick in the air.

"Mmmm," the goblin says. "Food pile make Itaa hungry."

I nearly vomit when she pulls a large maggot out of a gnome skull's eye socket and slurps it down. Then I look down at my hands and they are also covered in maggots and rotten flesh.

"No time for eat," Itaa says, staring at my hands as if she thought I was planning on eating the clumps of rot in my fingers.

She wipes the maggots out of my hands, and then helps me to my feet. She licks her fingers as we leave the room.

3: Owlbear Den

In this room, there is a sleeping **owlbear (AC5; HD 5+2; hp 29; #Att 3; Dmg 1d6 x2, 2d6)** chained to the wall. Itaa tells me the owlbear was put here by the gnolls to act as a guardian of the dungeon levels of Tardis Keep.

"Sneak," Itaa tells me.

She uses **Move Silently** to get along the outside of the wall toward the door. I follow her. Although the owlbear is chained, it has quite a bit of reach. The chain also doesn't look very strong. We wouldn't want to wake this creature. The two of us alone would not do very well against it, especially with Itaa unarmed.

1: Hallway

We escape the owlbear without waking it and enter an empty hallway. I go to the only door in the hall, assuming it leads upstairs.

"Not that way," Itaa says.

She leads me to the end of the hallway.

"Secret place," she says, as she feels along the north wall. When she hits the proper brick, the door slides open.

"Only Itaa knows here," she says. "This is Itaa's secret place."

Then she leads me inside and closes the secret door behind us.

2: Itaa's Room

Inside this room, there are small wooden chairs and a table, a bed of straw on a stone ledge, and boxes of preserved food.

"This Itaa's place," she says.

Then she explains how she hides in this room whenever she escapes the gnolls. She lived in the ruins of this keep with her people long before the gnolls moved in and took over. The gnolls killed most of her tribe, because they resisted. Itaa survived. This has been her secret room since she was a kid.

"What are we doing here?" I ask her. "Do you need to retrieve your belongings before we escape the keep?"

Itaa grunts. She pulls a suit of leather armor out of a chest and holds it up to her body.

"Need protection," she says.

I notice the armor doesn't look like the armor of a goblin. It is too well-constructed, intricately designed.

"Where did you get this armor?" I ask.

She looks at me with her blank yellow eyes and grins. "Halfgirl thief," she says. "She raid Itaa home for gold and Itaa kill with trap. Itaa take halfgirl armor."

It worries me to know that Itaa killed a female halfling to get this armor. It also is a pity, because judging by the shape of the clothing that halfling thief must have had an incredibly sexy body. I can imagine (or maybe it's my player and DM who are imagining) that she looked incredibly hot in that outfit. Much hotter than Itaa will probably look in it, that's for sure.

Itaa lays the leather outfit over her bed and then strips out of her clothing, not in the least bit shy to be naked in front of me. From behind, she actually has a nice body even though she's a goblin. The Dungeon Master explains her ass to my player in great detail. *Shiny green water balloons* is one of the many descriptions the DM gives to my player. While examining her body from behind, I realize how similar she looks to halfling females. Aside from the green skin, bald head and batwing-like ears, our races are not much different.

When she turns around, I notice that from the front her body is even more attractive. She has curvy hips and perky little breasts with green nipples. Itaa sees me ogling her body and smiles at me with sharp pointy little teeth.

"Itaa want Halfman, too," she says.

I back up, realizing what my player is trying to get me into.

"Itaa owe Halfman for giving Itaa freedom," she says.

Then she tosses her clothes down and leans seductively against her bed, sticking out her breasts and slightly spreading her legs to expose her vagina, its lips a darker shade of green.

"Shouldn't we get back to the others?" I ask.

She beckons me to come near her. "Itaa want Halfman."

I don't think I like where this is going. It is nothing new in my world to end up having sex with slutty humanoids all the time, but they are usually not goblinoids. I have slept with gnomes, dwarves, humans, dozens of elves (who always seem the sluttiest), and of course I've been raped by trolls, orcs, bugbears, and an ogre once shoved me up his ass. But I've never had sex with a goblin before, nor has any non-playable race of humanoid ever tried to seduce me.

Her glossy yellow eyes draw me toward her. I have to admit that I am kind of attracted to her. I'm sick of sleeping with humanoids that are bigger than me. I'm always being molested by humans and elves. At least this goblin is my size, perhaps even a little shorter.

When I come to her she pulls me up onto the bed and helps me out of my clothes. Then she kisses me gently with her dark green lips. At first I withdraw from her kiss, thinking her mouth will be putrid from her unhealthy diet of bugs and rotten meat, but she doesn't taste rotten. Her saliva is strong, but it is more of a pine flavor, and it gives me a stinging sensation when her forked tongue enters my mouth.

"Itaa like Halfman kiss," she says. "More soft than goblin."

Naked with the goblin girl in her straw bed, we wrap ourselves around each other, our kisses becoming more passionate. I suck on her green nipples and squeeze her firm goblin ass. She licks my back up to my shoulders, then curls her tongue into my armpits. She focuses on my armpits a lot, sucking on them and gently biting the soft under flesh, as if armpits are an erogenous area for goblins. I decide to reciprocate and lick her armpits, but not for very long because the taste is not to my liking. Her armpit sweat seems filled with intense goblin pheromones that taste like chili peppers. Next thing I know our foreplay heats up to the point that we attack each other, rolling around in the straw.

Then the goblin girl crawls to the middle of the bed and spreads her legs for me, rubbing her fingers inside of the deep green folds between her legs.

goblin fever

"Itaa Itaa," she says.

I'm not sure why she says that.

"Itaa!" she says, almost annoyed that I haven't already acted upon her command. "Itaa Itaa, Halfman!"

Then I realize what she's trying to say. Itaa is the goblin word for attack. She is trying to say attack Itaa. Itaa is probably an odd name even for a goblin. Her last name, Tohiish, means dangerous. So this means her name translates to: *Attack! Dangerous!*

The word itaa usually means to attack an opponent, but it might also be a goblin slang word for *fuck*. I believe she is saying *fuck Itaa*.

"Itaa Itaa!" she says to me, lifting her vagina in my direction and pointing at her crotch. "Fuck Itaa, Halfman!"

Well, she just said fuck, so maybe itaa isn't slang for fuck. Maybe she really did want me to attack her. With my penis? Not sure.

When we have sex, it is strange to me. Not because having sex with a goblin is weird, but because it actually feels right to me. It seems more natural than any other humanoid I've ever slept with. Perhaps it is her small size. But, no, I've had sex with gnomes before which are about the same height. This feels more natural than sex with any gnome. Her teeth are like needles against my tongue and her yellow eyes glow wide-open at me as she slides me in and out of her.

I believe she seduced me for a reason. She didn't want to reward me with sex for setting her free, she wanted to sleep with me so that I would protect her from my companions. She knows that they are likely to kill her once her usefulness has been used up. I bet she wants to fuck me as a means of persuasion, so that I won't let anything bad happen to her until we part ways. This kind of trickery is common among goblins, and using sex as a means of preservation is a common practice among goblin females.

But even though she likely had an agenda when we first

started engaging in sexual intercourse, I believe she might view things differently now. We have a powerful connection. There's this energy that I feel between us. We aren't just fucking, we are making love. I believe it is the first time I have ever made love since the day my player created me. It is new and . . . special. It is much better than the sex I've had before.

We moan loudly until we orgasm together. Then we curl up against one another, feeling each other's breaths against our bodies. I can feel Itaa almost purring against me, or maybe it is snoring. Whatever it is, it is very soothing.

Itaa wipes the saliva on her lips off onto my chest and stares into my eyes with her big yellow orbs.

"Itaa falling in like with Halfman," she says.

Then she rubs her hand up and down my body. The skin of her palm is smooth against my thigh, almost like the flesh of an amphibian. I wonder if falling in like is kind of like a precursor to falling in love.

"Halfman protect Itaa?" she asks.

Then I realize I was right, it was all just a trick for me to help her. She's just seduced me in order to use me. I sigh and nod my head.

"Halfman nice to Itaa," she says. "Itaa stay with Halfman."

Then she gives me a firm hug that I can swear has genuine emotion behind it, but there surely is not. She hops out of the bed and points her little green butt in my direction as she wiggles into her leather armor.

She actually does look cute in her leather armor. Not exactly as sexy as the armor was intended, but definitely cute. When she looks back at me lying in her bed, she gives me a big dumb smile. I can swear that I see a blissful glow emanating from her yellow eyes, the kind that you'd only get after sharing a passionate moment with the person you love. She has to be a brilliant actress.

1: Hallway

When we leave Itaa's room, we hear the owlbear roaring and squawking in area 3, its chains clinking against the floor.

The goblin girl says, "Itaa moan too loud. Bearowl wake up."

Then she giggles and hugs my arm close to her chest.

"Follow Itaa," she says, smiling and poking at me. "Sex take too long. Boobelf might be mad."

Then she leads me through the door to a stairwell. We hurry up the stairs back to the ground floor.

tardis keep

entry
level

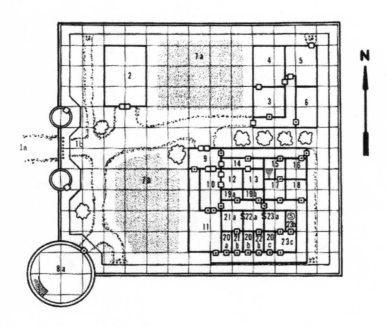

15: Library

I realize Itaa is still hugging my arm when we reach the top of the stairs and enter an old library. The books all seem to have been left here from the days when the keep was used by Lord Tennant, but now most of the books have withered from mildew and rot.

Itaa presses against me a little too tightly, caressing my back. I don't know what the others are going to think when they see us together. It would be embarrassing if they figure out that we just had sex. It would be even more embarrassing if they knew I might possibly be developing some feelings for the weird little green girl.

I pause for a moment and wonder what the hell is going on with my player and Dungeon Master. They have just roleplayed an oddly emotional sex scene between myself and the goblin girl. It is one thing for them to roleplay sex scenes in an attempt to be funny (like the bugbear butt-fucking the orc) or roleplay sex in order to vent some sexual frustration (like my threeway with the elf girls). But roleplaying a passionate sex scene? That is just strange.

Back in the real world, I can tell Mark thought it was pretty weird as well. Aaron is moving on with the game, as if it were not awkward and strange that he was pretending to be the goblin girl while making love to his friend's character. Mark tries to just move on with the game, but I can tell he is feeling uncomfortable. Mark always feels uncomfortable around Aaron.

At school, Mark doesn't hang out with his Dungeons and Dragons friends. In fact, he is ashamed of his friends and will never admit to anyone else that he plays D&D. Mark is a shy kid. He doesn't make friends very easily. He is usually intimidated by other people because of his size. Short, thin, and baby-faced, he is often mistaken as a child who skipped several grades rather than a teenager with stunted growth.

The only reason Mark ever became friends with Buzz and Aaron was because they were the only people to offer him their friendship. They saw him as one of them, an outsider. However, Mark is a different kind of outsider. He sees himself as more of a goth or a metal kid, even if he doesn't hang out with the goth/metal kids. He would do anything to break his friendship with them and join a different group of friends.

Lately, Mark has been smoking clove cigarettes under the bleachers with a kid he talks to in math class. This kid, Chris, is a year older than him and listens to the same bands. They don't talk outside of school, just during math class and when they smoke cloves. Mark would really like to hang out with Chris more and perhaps become a part of his crowd, but Chris hangs out with seniors, several of which have made fun of Mark in the past due to his size. He doesn't think they would ever let him into their clique. He is too timid to even try.

Whereas Mark is very concerned about his social standing in his school, Aaron Donnelly doesn't care what anybody thinks of him. Aaron is the fattest kid in school. He is so large that he has to use a wheelchair to get around. Aaron's parents got him the wheelchair after he had a heart attack last year, the first kid to ever have a heart attack in their junior high school (let alone the high school). He had it during PE class, when the militaristic PE coach forced him to run the mile in the hot Arizona heat.

Known as the least desirable male in the school, not only due to his horrible acne, thick glasses, grotesque weight, and wheelchair, but also due to his Dungeons and Dragons obsession. In school, Aaron wears a wizard hat and elf ears everywhere he goes, and has a long blue cape with silver glitter that he calls his Cloak of Displacement. Not only that, but he custom designed his wheelchair (with construction paper) to look like a mighty warhorse, with painted cardboard legs dangling from the armrests in front of the wheels, and a tail on the back of his seat. Above the tail on the back of the chair is a picture of a flaming 20-sided die with swords crossed beneath it, kind of like a skull and bones pirate flag.

Since Todd and Buzz have different lunch hours as the two of them, Aaron always wants to hang out with Mark. Every day, Mark tries to ditch him. He doesn't want anybody to know they are friends and if anybody ever asks he always denies it. Mark always brings his lunch from home so that he doesn't have to eat in the cafeteria. Immediately after 5th period, he hides behind the music building and eats his lunch, hoping that Aaron doesn't find him back there.

Aaron has no idea that Mark is embarrassed by him, nor does he realize that Mark tries to avoid him at lunchtime. Even when Mark runs in the opposite direction when they see each other, Aaron just assumes Mark hasn't seen him yet. Mark walks as fast as he can in the other direction, with Aaron speeding after him in his wheelchair, his Cloak of Displacement flapping in the wind.

These are the most embarrassing times for Mark. Aaron chases him through the hallway, not able to take a hint, yelling, "Dragonblade! Come forth!"

Dragonblade is Aaron's nickname for Mark. He gave him this name because he once played a character, long before I was created, called Lance Dragonblade. The character died at level 22, but the nickname stuck.

Mark's face cringes every time he hears Aaron's voice screaming "Dragonblade!" from down the hall. The sound of the wheelchair whirring across carpet toward him is the sound of impending doom.

Aaron always yells something like, "Dragonblade! I cast **Hold Person** upon thee! Freeze in thy tracks and await your wizard friend!" Then he holds up two cans of Dr. Pepper. "I bought a Potion of Healing for you! Why can't you hear me, you little quickling?"

Everyone in the school always stares at Mark whenever this happens. Although he is too embarrassed to look anyone in the eyes, he swears they are all laughing at him. Sometimes he hates Aaron with every bone in his body. Even more than that, he hates himself for becoming such a nerd.

17: Olffgel's Room

This room belongs to the gnome wizard Olffgel Zookwar, who works with the Gnoll King. Olffgel offers his magical services to the king in exchange for protection, supplies, a place to live, and a laboratory. This room is vacant at the moment. Itaa tells me the wizard is usually in his underground laboratory. He only comes out to sleep or when called upon by the Gnoll King. Itaa has had to serve him food in the laboratory many times in the past, which she says she always hated doing because of the unpleasant nature of the gnome wizard.

"Itaa hate dirty old gnome," she says.

We open the **Wizard Locked** door and find Loxi, Juzii, and Delvok sitting in the hall, bored out of their minds.

"Finally!" Juzii says.

"What took you so long?" Loxi asks. "Were you two fucking or something?"

Then she laughs, like she had just said a cruel joke at my expense. At first I thought she said it because she could tell that we did actually just have sex, but then I realize she was just teasing and doesn't have a clue. She might think the idea of the goblin girl and I having sex is completely absurd.

As they enter the room, I see somebody else coming down the hall toward us. The person waves his arm. The others turn around to see who it is.

"It is I," he says. "The Dwaaaaarf Looooord! The slayer of gnolls!"

All of our jaws go slack.

"You're still alive?" I ask.

He enters the room and we close the door behind him.

"Aye!" he says. "I killed every last gnoll with my berserker rage! And then I ran into a party of filthy gnomes and axed them down too!"

"You killed the gnomes?" I yell. "They were just women and children! We planned to rescue them!"

"The little buggers got in me way!" Dwarfy says.

Then the dwarf moves on past us toward the library. Luckly, he didn't notice the goblin girl hiding behind me, or else he would have tried to cut her head off.

"What are yea waiting for, you cowards!" he says, as he leaves the room. "Let us continue on to battle!"

I turn to Delvok. "How the heck did he survive that battle? Last we saw of him, he had only one hit point left."

Delvok looks to me. "It is highly improbable, but he must have killed the rest of the gnolls without losing any more hit points. All of the gnolls' attack rolls must have failed."

"But he has an armor class of 8 and they have a hit dice of 2," I say. "Rolling anything higher than a 10 would beat him. How can so many gnoll attacks roll so low against one dwarf?"

"He did use berserker rage," Delvok says. "It is improbable, but not impossible, that he would survive."

I shake my head, assuming that the Dungeon Master went easy on his brother's character to keep him in the game longer. We follow the others back into the library.

15: Library

In the library, Juzii is searching through the books for anything useful. Most of the books are very old and the pages crumble in her hands.

"Anything valuable?" Loxi asks her elf friend.

Juzii shakes her head for a second, and then her eyes light up. "Wait a minute!"

She pulls a scroll from the shelf and examines it.

"What's that?" Loxi asks.

"Nice," Juzii says. "A scroll of **Detect Invisibility**. This might come in handy."

She puts it in her bag.

"Kind of a boring treasure," Loxi says.

"You never know," Juzii says. "We might need it. If not I bet we could sell it at a decent price."

"I guess . . ." Loxi says.

Juzii sticks her tongue out as we descend the stairs into the dungeon levels.

magic sex shop inventory

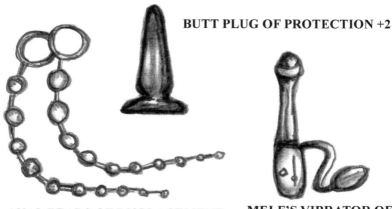

BUTT PLUG OF PROTECTION +2

ANAL BEADS OF DISPLACEMENT

MELF'S VIBRATOR OF ETERNAL ORGASMS

OGRE SCHLONG

COCK RING OF INVISIBILITY

BLOW-UP SEX DOLL (ELF)

FLOG OF ELECTRIC SHOCK (20 CHARGES)

POCKET PUSSY OF LUBRICATION

tardis keep

dungeon
level

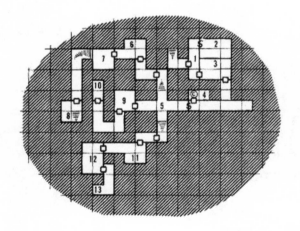

1: Hallway

The Dwarf Lord swings his axe around as we enter the hall. He attacks an unlit torch on one of the walls until it is just pieces on the floor.

"It is good we have The Dwarf Lord with us again," Delvok says.

I was thinking just the opposite.

"He is the most powerful warrior of our party," Delvok says. "We wouldn't go very far without him."

"Yeah, but he has only one hit point left," I say. "He might not last much longer."

Delvok nods. "We must find a way to heal him as soon as possible, before he gets himself killed."

3: Owlbear Den

When The Dwarf Lord sees the owlbear chained to the wall in the chamber, he raises his axe and charges straight for the creature.

He lets out his battlecry, "Prepare to taste the steel of the—"

The owlbear bites his head off.

The dwarf's headless body falls to the ground. We all stare blankly as the owlbear tears meat from his corpse.

"That was kind of stupid," I say.

"I believe we should have convinced him to avoid fighting until after we found him some health," Delvok says.

"Yeah," I say, watching the owlbear tear into our ex-companion's stomach with its large beak.

In the real world, Todd leaves Aaron's room and heads off for bed, almost as if he got himself killed on purpose because he was bored with the game. Mark is happy to see him go, but I can tell that Aaron preferred having his brother around. Dungeons and Dragons is just more fun with four players.

5: Corridor

We return to the corridor where Itaa and I first arrived in the dungeon. Itaa shows us how to get through the secret door and leads us into the rest of the dungeon area.

We come to a crossroads, with passages leading in four directions.

"Which way should we go?" Juzii asks.

"Stairs to lower dungeon," Itaa says, pointing north.

"We don't want to go down there yet," Loxi says. "We want to explore the area first. Find some valuables."

Itaa nods.

We decide to take the south passage. As we descend some stairs, I hear footsteps behind us.

"Does anyone hear that?" I ask.

Everyone stops and listens. They don't hear anything. We continue moving. I hear more footsteps, like there are a dozen of us rather than just five.

We stop again.

"I heard it too that time," Juzii says.

Loxi shakes her head. "It's just the echo."

We continue on, and stop again, the footsteps seem to be out of sync with ours. We move more quickly until we get to a door.

"I think you might be right," Loxi says. "Let's get out of here."

11: Deserted Chamber

We run inside of a vacant room. Loxi tries to close the door behind her, but it won't shut, as if the door is jammed open. After using all of her strength, the door slams shut.

"What the hell was that?" Loxi says, out of breath.

She leans against the wall and continues to breathe hard from using all her energy to close the door. Her breath echoes through the room, sounding as if several people are breathing heavy all at the same time.

"Wait a minute . . ." I say, listening carefully to the heavy breathing.

"What?" Loxi says.

When she spoke, the heavy breathing didn't stop with her.

"Be quiet," I say. "Listen."

We listen carefully, not making a noise, but we hear sounds all around us. Breathing sounds, smacking sounds, whimpering sounds.

"We're not alone in here," Juzii says.

Loxi gets up and draws her sword. "Fuck."

I turn to Juzii. "Use your scroll."

"**Detect Invisibility**?" she asks. "You think there's something invisible in here?"

"Yeah," I say.

"But I just got this scroll," she says. "I don't want to use it yet."

"Just do it," Loxi says.

Juzii shakes her head as she unrolls the parchment. "Fine."

She reads the incantation on the scroll and the spell goes into effect. Slowly, seven figures come into view as their invisibility becomes detected. We point our weapons at them, prepared for battle.

When the figures become clear, we fall back. The figures are seven elderly men. All of them are masturbating furiously, staring at Loxi's nude breasts.

"What the fuck?" Loxi says.

The men don't realize we can see them. They just continue masturbating and licking their lips.

"Have these guys been following us around this whole time?" Juzii asks. "Watching us while invisible?"

"They saw when we had sex?" I ask, meaning when I had sex with Loxi and Juzii, not with Itaa.

"Ewwwww," Loxi says, cringing at the elderly men.

She shakes her hands as if trying to shake the dirty thoughts out of her head. The old men masturbate more furious when she shakes her hands, because the movement makes her boobs bounce up and down.

"Can we make them invisible again?" I ask.

Juzii shakes her head. "Just got to wait until the spell wears off."

"How long will that be?" Loxi says.

"A while," Juzii says.

A long pause. We just stare at them for a few moments as

they masturbate in our direction.

"Sooooo," I say, breaking the awkward silence. "Now what?"

"Uhhh," Juzii says. "Wait until they disappear again, I guess."

"So are they going to keep following us around for the rest of the quest?" I say. "Invisibly masturbating while watching us?"

Long pause.

"Don't know," Loxi says. "Don't want to know."

The rest of them agree.

We continue to watch the dirty old men as they fade away. Instead of going on to area 12, we decide to backtrack and go in another direction. After seeing the old men, we decide this area of the dungeon is bad luck.

5: Corridor

We return to the crossroads and this time decide to take the western passage. As we walk, I ask Itaa about the old men.

"Ever see them before?" I ask.

She shrugs. "Probably Olffgel friends."

"Olffgel has perverted wizard friends?" I ask.

"Olffgel more big pervert wizard than all," she says.

Then she tells me the story of the gnome wizard Olffgel Zookwar. He is the most perverted wizard that has ever existed across the land, possessing more fetishes than even Loxi. The only reason he became a wizard in the first place was to use his magic for sex. At first, he used spells like **Enlarge**, just to enhance his penis size. Then he would cast Haste so that he could have sex with women at a faster pace.

Then he started getting a little kinky. He would cast **Web** for bondage sex. He would cast **Invisibility** on prostitutes, because he had a fetish for having sex with invisible people. He would cast **Mirror Image** and masturbate to the illusionary clones of himself that surround him, who also masturbated back at him.

Then he got sexually abusive with his magic. He used **Clairvoyance** to explore his voyeur fetish, and watched women going to the bathroom, bathing in the nude from a distance, or watched couples having sex. He would cast **Hold Person** on people and then steal their clothes, to get off on their embarrassment as they ran naked through the streets. Then he started to cast **Sleep** on women and have his way with them. **Sleep** is the ultimate date rape spell.

Then he started getting beyond perverted with his magic. He would cast **Summon Animal** to fulfill his bestiality fetish. Then he would cast **Feign Death** on women to do his necrophilia fetish. Later, his necrophilia fetish turned into a zombie fetish, so he learned **Animate Dead** to bring corpses to life which he commanded to bend over for him. Then he would cast **Magic Mouth** on inanimate objects such as trees and chairs, so that he could force the mouth that would appear on these objects to give him blowjobs. The idea of receiving a blowjob from a couch or a lamp was a big turn on for him.

The wizard is continually studying magic and learning new spells, for the sole purpose of using them in strange sex acts. This does not make him an incredibly powerful wizard, because he does not bother with any attack spells or defense spells. Still, I hope I never have the misfortune of meeting such a wizard.

a gnome wizard
getting a blowjob from
a 1964 vw bug using

magic mouth

9: Guest Room

We find it rather odd to come across a guest room in the middle of a dungeon. The room is very clean in comparison to the other places we've been to, including most of the rooms on the ground floor. The bed is heart-shaped with red silk sheets.

"This is kind of odd," I say.

Loxi calls everyone into the room and then locks the door behind her.

"What did you do that for?" I ask.

"I don't want the perverted old men coming in after us," she says.

"Why's that?" I ask.

She points at the bed. "Because I didn't want them to watch our orgy."

I shake my head and step away from her. "No, no. Not again. We just had sex."

Loxi takes Juzii aside and they whisper to each other, coming up with a game plan, a sinister grin on her face when she looks over at me and Delvok.

I take Delvok to the corner to complain.

"I can't believe our goddamn perverted Dungeon Master," I say. "I want to get on with our quest but all I'm ever doing is having sex with these girls. I already had a threesome with the elf girls and just a handful of turns ago I found myself in bed with Itaa for no reason."

"You had sex with the goblin?" Delvok asks, raising an eyebrow.

"It's getting annoying," I say.

I can tell Delvok doesn't share my annoyance too much,

because he has yet to have any sex on this quest.

When the elf girls approach us, Juzii chooses Delvok and Loxi chooses me. Itaa pulls me away from Loxi before she can kiss me. Then she gets between us, growling.

"What's with you, little troll?" Loxi says. "You have a crush on my little boy or something?"

Itaa just growls at her again.

Delvok is very excited to have sex with Juzii and already has an erection. That is, until she casts **Change Self** and becomes a hermaphrodite harpy with a 16" penis. She squawks loudly and claws off his armor, then wraps her wings around him.

"We're going to go find a private place," Juzii says, rubbing her boner against Delvok's lower back. "I'm going to fuck this elf silly."

Delvok struggles within Juzii's harpy wings.

"I find the use of your **Change Self** spell highly illogical," Delvok says, his eyebrows cringing downward as Juzii's penis squeezes into his asshole. He tries to compose himself without showing pain, and continues with a groaning voice. "When using a spell to enhance the act of coupling, it would be more logical to alter your appearance to become a more attractive mate, not a less attractive one."

Juzii laughs. "I didn't cast the spell for your benefit."

She slowly pulls her penis out of him, then slams it back in.

"Sorry," she says. "I'm getting ahead of myself."

She looks over at us. "Have fun. We'll see you later."

She opens the southern door, lifts Delvok off the ground, and flies down the hallway. I can see her hips thrusting into Delvok's ass, fucking him as she flies. I might have already had some weird sex on this quest, but at least I didn't get anything shoved up my ass. The Dungeon Master really has a thing for shoving things up people's asses.

Loxi turns on me now.

a harpy
with a dick

"Looks like we're alone," she says.

Then she feels a thud and looks down. Itaa is pushing on her belly.

"Boobelf no fuck Halfman," Itaa says.

Loxi has no idea what she is saying.

"At first I thought your little crush was kind of cute," Loxi says to her. "Now it's getting annoying."

"No Boobelf," Itaa says.

Loxi speaks slow to the goblin, as if that might help her understand what she's saying. "You can have sex with him, too. We can share him."

Itaa growls at her. I'm beginning to think the goblin might actually like me. I know goblins are very territorial creatures, but it's kind of strange seeing her act so territorial about me. After the elf recognizes the serious look in the goblin's eyes, she gives up.

"Fine, I'll just watch," Loxi says.

The elf grabs my Bag of Holding and pulls out some rope.

"She really likes you." Loxi smiles at me. "I'm sorry for doing this, but I just have to let her have her way with you."

Then Loxi grabs me and pulls off my clothes. Itaa punches her on the back with her tiny green fists.

"Hey, I'm trying to help you," Loxi says, pushing the green girl to the ground.

Then Loxi ties me to the heart-shaped bed and backs away before Itaa attacks her again. Itaa gets in her face and growls up at her, threatening her with her long goblin claws. Loxi raises her arms in surrender.

"I won't touch him, you little scrote," she says.

Itaa continues to growl, backing away from Loxi and holding out her arms to prevent the elf from getting past her.

"You can fuck him," Loxi says. "I want to see what it's like for a goblin to fuck a halfling."

I'm pretty surprised Loxi hasn't realized that I have already had sex with the goblin. By the way Itaa is acting toward me, how long we took to get back to them after we went off alone together, and how Itaa is now wearing different clothes than she used to be wearing, you'd think Loxi would have put the clues together.

While looking at Itaa in her tight leather armor, I realize that my penis is becoming erect.

"Awww, how cute," Loxi says. "He's already hard for you."

Loxi points at my penis and Itaa turns to see my erection. She examines it carefully with her yellow eyes, then looks back at Loxi.

"Yeah," Loxi says. "It's for you."

Loxi points again and Itaa looks back again.

"Now, go get it," Loxi says, speaking to her like she's a dog. "Go get it, girl!"

Itaa inches toward me but won't turn her back on the elf. She hesitates, probably because she has no idea what the elf is trying to communicate to her.

"Go get him!" Loxi says, pushing the goblin at the bed.

Itaa turns around and hisses like a cat. Then continues growling as she climbs up on the bed next to me. She looks cautiously back at Loxi, not sure what she has planned.

"Crazy Boobelf," Itaa says.

Loxi smiles as she sees Itaa near me.

"Now fuck him," she says. "Fuck him good, you goblin slut."

"Boobelf no fuck Halfman," Itaa says to me. "Only Itaa fuck Halfman now."

I tell her, "She only wants to watch."

Itaa looks back at Loxi.

"Only Itaa fuck Halfman?" says the goblin girl. "Boobelf only watch?"

"Yeah," I say. "She wants to watch you fuck me."

Itaa smiles wide and bounces up and down on the bed like a childish gremlin, she even smiles giddily at Loxi with

128

her tiny needle teeth.

"Itaa fuck Halfman!" she says. Then she feels the ropes and my naked body. "Halfman tied. Halfman at Itaa mercy."

Then she bounces on the bed even more excited. This is really becoming a turn off for me.

"Yeah, now you're getting into the right spirit!" Loxi says, watching Itaa as she takes off her leather armor. "He's all yours. Have your way with him!"

Then Loxi laughs as Itaa lunges at me like a playful kitten and fiercely licks my chest and armpits.

"I'm so sorry," Loxi says to me, giggling and shaking her head. "You're going to hate me for doing this to you, but it's just so damned adorable. She really does like you. I just had to let her have her way with you."

Itaa rubs her naked body against mine, messaging my penis between her bony green fingers, making purring noises against me.

"Awww, you have a new girlfriend," Loxi says, giggling as the goblin cuddles against me. "To tell you the truth, you two actually do make a pretty cute couple."

Itaa gets on top of me and puts me inside of her, she digs her claws into my shoulders as she bounces rapidly on top of me. I look around her green hips at Loxi, who now has her pants down. She licks her fingers and then begins to masturbate as she watches the goblin have her way with me.

"Oh, yeah," Loxi says, moaning with her eyes locked on the two of us. "Fuck his tiny halfling dick."

Itaa moves my face away from Loxi's direction so that I'm looking into her eyes. Her mouth is wide open as she fucks me, her forked tongue curling around her bottom lip. As she comes closer to orgasm, her tiny nose wrinkles up into a snarl. For a moment, it looks as if she is about to bite into my flesh with her pointy teeth and rip my throat out, but she just stares at me. She just absorbs me into her glowing monsterous eyes.

I look back at Loxi and notice her pulling something out

of my Bag of Holding.

"Don't do that!" I yell at Loxi, as I see the Dildo of Enlightenment +2 enter her vagina.

"Yeah, fuck him you goblin slut . . ." Loxi says as she masturbates with the dildo.

"You don't know what you're doing," I cry. "Take it out! Take it out now!"

Instead, Loxi climbs naked onto the bed with us, licking her lips. She masturbates furiously with the dildo at the foot of the bed.

"The dildo is bad!" I say. "It's bad magic!"

Sensing the elf is on the bed with us, Itaa growls loudly at the intruder as she fucks me, but she is so close to orgasm that she's not able to stop.

Loxi slips the dildo out of her vagina, and just as Itaa and I cum together, Loxi shoves the dildo up the goblin girl's asshole.

Itaa shrieks and jumps off of me, flying off of the bed and running around the room with the dildo stuck up her butt. She thinks she's been attacked.

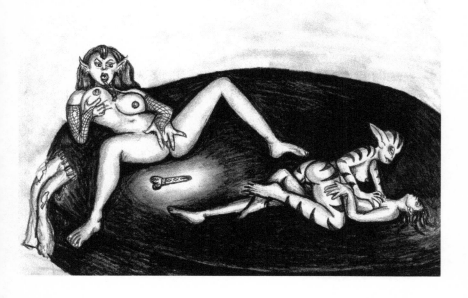

"Untie me," I tell Loxi.

Loxi is looking down at her lap, rubbing her head. A look of dread is slowly crossing her face. Itaa stops running and looks behind her at the thing sticking out of her backside. She hisses at her butt, as if the dildo is a living thing biting her. When she pulls it out, she holds it up and frowns at it, confused about what it is or where it came from.

Loxi looks up at me with panic on her face, her mouth wide open like she has tons of things to tell me but can't get any words out. Then, slowly, the same look of shock appears on Itaa's face.

"I'm not real?" Loxi says to me, her eyes beginning to water. "We're just characters in some stupid game?"

The goblin girl frowns at me and sits down on the bed.

"Itaa sad now," she says.

Loxi says, "I'm just a goddamn fucking made up character!"

"Welcome to my life," I tell her. "I told you not to use the dildo."

"But I'm not even a player character," Loxi says. "I'm just a fucking NPC! I'm not being role-played by an actual player in the game. I'm just a side character whose sole purpose is to give boners to horny little dorks!" Then she looks down at her chest. "No wonder why my boobs are so big!" Then she says, "And no wonder why I walk around topless!"

I give her a look of condolence. It's bad enough being a player character. I couldn't imagine what it's like for her, being one of many non player characters that are controlled by Aaron Donnelly.

"Itaa just monster," Itaa cries. "Itaa only invented for PCs to kill and get experience points." Itaa frowns and lays her chin on my naked chest, looking up at me with sad puppy dog eyes.

She says in a half-crying voice, "Itaa no special at all."

I pet Itaa's bald green head.

Loxi puts her pants back on. Then she pulls out her broad

sword and slices a piece of red fabric from the sheet.

"What are you doing?" I ask.

Loxi cuts a hole in the middle of the piece of fabric and slides her head through.

"I'm not going topless anymore," she says.

Then she cuts a strip of fabric from the sheet and uses it as a belt to tie around her midsection to keep the sides of her new shirt closed.

"You sure that's a good idea?" I ask. "They created you to be a sexy slutty elf chick. If you stop they might get bored of you and kill you off."

"I'm not letting anyone kill me off," she says.

"They always kill off the NPCs," I say. "Every quest I have gone on there have always been NPCs whose sole purpose is to fuck us and then get killed off along the way."

"I'm not playing their game anymore," she says.

"You don't have a choice," I say. "The Dungeon Master controls you."

"Fuck the Dungeon Master," she says.

She grabs the Dildo of Enlightenment +2 and goes to the door to the south.

"Where are you going?" I ask.

"Juzii needs to know, too," she says.

I jump out of the bed.

"You sure she wants to know?" I yell out of the doorway, pulling my chainmail on.

Itaa curls up in the bed with her green butt in the air, saying, "Itaa sad. Big sad."

I gather my belongings and follow after Loxi, leaving Itaa in the bed.

10: Frog Room

The inside of this room is filled with large aquariums holding various reptiles and amphibians. The aquariums along the side of the walls are filled with smaller snakes and lizards, but on the north wall there is one large aquarium filled with tall green plants, rocks, and waterfalls.

Delvok and Juzii are nowhere to be seen, but their clothes and belongings are scattered across the floor. Loxi looks carefully at the aquarium and notices the front pane of glass has been completely shattered. Camouflaged behind the vegetation, we discover the occupant of the glass cage: a **giant frog (AC7; HD 2; hp 18; #Att 1; Dmg 1-3/1-6/2-8, SA swallow).**

Then I notice Delvok, naked, hiding in the corner of the room between the snake cages. I go to him.

"What happened?"

He points at the frog's belly and we see movement coming from within. Hands are pushing out on its stretchy skin, trying to get out. Then Delvok tells me about how they were in the middle of having sex when the frog broke through the cage and attacked the harpy with its long pink tongue. Then, in an instant, the frog sucked her into her mouth like a fly and swallowed her whole.

Loxi panics when she hears her friend's voice crying for help within the frog belly.

"We need to get her out of there," Loxi says, drawing her sword.

The frog hops out of the aquarium toward us. I draw my short sword +1 and attack. Right off the bat, I get a critical hit but only roll a 2+1, doing 6 points of damage. Loxi hits him too, but only takes off 1 point. Loxi is in tears as she swings her sword, but I'm not sure if it is because she's terrified of losing her friend or because of her new perspective of the universe.

The frog attacks me but misses. Delvok goes for his bow and aims his arrow at the creature, joining this fight naked with his bald elven balls stuck to the side of his cum-drenched thigh. His attack roll fails. Within the belly of the frog, Juzii attacks with a kick. It only does 1 point of damage, though. She had been swallowed with no weapons or armor. The frog's digestive juices do 2d8 points of damage to Juzii as she squirms in the creature's stomach.

Loxi attacks furiously, but misses. I stab at its belly, careful not to hit Juzii within, doing 4 more points of damage. Delvok fires an arrow and it lands in the frog's face, doing 5 more points of damage.

The frog attacks me with its tongue, trying to eat me like it did Juzii, probably thinking I'm the easiest meal because of my size. The tongue hits me for 2 points of damage, not killing me but knocking me off of my feet.

2d8 more points of damage to Juzii. Her movements slow inside of the creature's stomach. I'm not worried about her being digested to death by the frog. I'm worried about her dying of asphyxiation. She probably only has one round left of oxygen in there. If we don't kill the thing within the next round she will die. Luckily the creature has only 2 hit points left. Just one of us has to land a blow.

Delvok fires an arrow but gets a critical miss. The arrow breaks in half as he pulls back on the bow, the splinters piercing him in the chest for 1 point of damage and he loses a round. I swing my sword and miss, rolling only a 5+1. It's up to Loxi. She sees Juzii go limp inside of the creature's stomach, her hand sliding down into the acids. With her last chance, Loxi swings her broad sword with all of her might and stabs the creature in the face. It falls backward, its tongue flying out of its mouth.

But it doesn't die. Loxi only did 1 point of damage. It still has one more HP. And instead of using its last breath to attack, the giant frog flees. It hops back into the aquarium. Loxi chases after it, but the thing jumps into the pond in the back of the aquarium. It swims down to the bottom and squeezes its large blobby frame into an underwater cave.

"What the fuck!" Loxi yells at the edge of the pond. "Get back here you motherfucker!"

Inside of the frog, Juzii takes her last breath as the digestive fluid consumes her. The last thing she feels is the sensation of her skin melting down the sides of her body.

"I'm going to kill you, you fucking frog!" Loxi screams.

I go to her.

"Come on," I say, pulling her by the wrist.

She breaks my grasp.

"That son of a bitch needs to come up for air some time," she says. "I'll be here when it does."

"She's already dead," I tell her.

"I don't care," she says. "I'm going to kill that thing anyway."

135

"Leave it," I say. "She's gone. Let's just get out of here."

She pushes me away from her and I go to Delvok to help him pack up his belongings as he gets dressed. We wait with Loxi for a few rounds, but the frog never comes up for air. For all we know the thing bled to death down there or has a pocket of air on the ceiling of the cave, enough to last him the rest of the day.

Loxi stays for a while longer, not to wait for the frog but to mourn her dead friend. Then we leave the room to return to Itaa. I wouldn't tell this to Loxi, but it is almost for the best that Juzii died now. If Loxi had forced her to use the Dildo of Enlightenment +2 she would have had a horrible life from here on out. Knowing that you aren't real is no way to live a life.

9: Guest Room

Itaa is still lying in the bed, buried in the red silk sheets. It looks like she cried herself to sleep, unable to deal with her reality. I crawl into bed with her and put her head in my lap. We explain to Delvok about what happened with Itaa, Loxi, and the Dildo of Enlightenment +2. His eyebrows raise with interest, knowing that we no longer have to keep our knowledge a secret now that all of us in the party are aware of our circumstance.

"Now what?" I say to the others.

"It is not logical to continue this quest," Delvok says. "With only the three of us, we do not stand much of a chance against the Gnoll King."

"I agree," Loxi says. "This is all bullshit. We need to get back to town, where it's safe."

"Our players won't let us do that," I say. "They want us

to continue our mission."

"Yes, they would have more amusement playing until we are all dead than bringing us safely back to town."

"Why do you have to do what the players want?" Loxi says. "Just do what *you* want. Fuck what they tell you to do."

"That would be impossible," Delvok says. "Every single action we make is what players command of us."

"So we have absolutely no free will?" Loxi says. "Not a single action we make is our own?"

"Not one," says Delvok.

Loxi shakes her head. "So you're telling me right now that Buzz, Aaron, and Mark are the ones telling us what to say? They are sitting around a table roleplaying this exact conversation?"

"That is likely the case," says Delvok.

"Bullshit," Loxi says. "Why would they bother doing that? We are the ones having this conversation, not them. That means we do have some will of our own."

"So you think we can resist our players?" I ask. "Break their control of us and live our own life, with our own free will?"

Loxi nods. "That's what I believe."

"Or is it the Dungeon Master who is commanding you to believe that?" Delvok says. "He could have been the one who controlled you to use the dildo and then use it on the goblin. He might have thought it would be interesting to roleplay your character with this knowledge."

Loxi's face contorts into a mess when trying to fathom the idea of being completely controlled in every possible way by some kid in another world.

After some moments of silence, I say, "So what should we do?"

"Get out of the Keep," Loxi says. "Get far away from here."

"Perhaps it would be the most logical action to take given

the circumstances," Delvok says.

I shake my head at them.

"Delvok," I say. "You're forgetting something."

Delvok raises his eyebrows in question.

"Glimworm," I say. "The whole reason we went on this quest was to get some money so that we could get out of this region and away from him."

Delvok nods twice and then looks down at his feet.

I turn to Loxi. "The Dildo of Enlightenment +2 belongs to a kobold wizard named Glimworm. We took a quest to retrieve the magical item for him, but then…"

I'm not sure I want to mention what happened next.

Delvok interjects for me. "Due to circumstances beyond our control we were . . . injected . . . with the knowledge of our false existence."

"But the problem is," I continue, "Glimworm told us that he would kill us if we used the dildo. He is likely after us now, because he wants to get the dildo back and because he wants us dead."

"It is logical to assume that he believes no being should possess this knowledge," Delvok says.

"He probably knows we'd be better off dead," I say.

"So he's going to kill me now, too?" Loxi asks.

I nod. "And Itaa."

"Great," Loxi says, rolling her eyes. "Just what I needed."

"So I think we should continue the quest," I say. "We should try to avoid any fight we can, but we need to find the treasure room. Or any treasure room. Once we have enough gold we can get out and travel far away from here."

"With only the three of us?" Loxi asks.

"Four," I say. "We have Itaa, too."

"Great," she says. "A fucking goblin is going to do a lot of good. She's just a grunt that won't even last long against level 1 players."

"She's a level 2 ranger," I say. "She's more than just

an average goblin."

"Well, I guess she's better than nothing," Loxi says.

"She also knows her way around the dungeon," I say.

"Fine, let's take her," she says. "Let's get moving. The sooner we get some gold and get out of this place the better."

We all agree.

I wake up Itaa and give her the leather armor. She wipes her yellow eyes languidly as she pulls on the tight halfling clothes. Then I hand her bow to her. She looks up at me with questioning eyes.

"Give Itaa bow?" she asks, taking the weapon.

"We want you to join us on our mission," I tell her. "Can we trust you?"

"Boobelf and Trekelf now Itaa friend?" she asks.

"Yes," I say. "They're your friends now."

"No kill Itaa?" she asks.

"No, you're our friend now," I say. "You're like us. You understand what we really are."

She lowers her head and says quietly. "Itaa understand now. Itaa just Dungeons and Dragons monster. Weak small monster."

I put my arm on her shoulder. "So, are you with us?"

She looks up and wipes a tear from her eye, then smiles.

"Itaa stay with Halfman," she says, placing both of her hands on top of my wrist. "Trust Itaa."

5: Corridor

We return to the crossroads in the hallway and take the northern passage. We don't hear any invisible masturbating wizards. They must have gone off to masturbate to something else in Tardis Keep. Knowing our Dungeon Master, there are probably tons of jerk-worthy things happening in other parts of the castle that would be perfect for them.

Loxi pulls out a dagger and holds it out to the goblin girl.

"Here," Loxi says, handing the knife over to her. "You might need a melee weapon in addition to your bow."

Itaa takes the knife and examines it, admiring its shine in the torchlight. Goblins are used to seeing only dull, rusted blades.

She smiles and looks at me.

"Boobelf Itaa friend," she says, putting the knife through her belt loop.

I smile back and continue walking. Her excitement to be among new friends seems incredibly genuine to me. The way she acts could not be faked. However, that doesn't mean that she won't turn on us. She is still being played by Aaron Donnelly, who might force her to stab me in the back just for the fun of it. Unless, that is, Loxi is right and we really can make our own choices if we want. Perhaps we can break free of our players and live our lives the way we choose.

6: Statue Room

This room is filled with statues of naked ogres with giant boners. Some of the statues are masturbating these boners or sticking them into other statues. One statue is balancing a Wand of Magic Missiles on the tip of its penis head.

"This might prove useful," Delvok says, as he removes the wand. "I am part magic-user, after all."

Then the statue comes to life and becomes a **stone guardian (AC: 2, HD 4+4, hp 21, #AT 1, D 2-9).** The living statue breaks off its boner and uses it as a large club. Before Delvok can react, it slams the stone boner down onto the elf's skull, breaking open his head. It does 4 hit points of damage, leaving Delvok with 1 HP left.

"Run!" I yell at Delvok.

Itaa and Loxi think I'm speaking to them and they take off to area 7. Delvok uses his round to escape, but the stone ogre moves just as fast as an elf. I run to area 7, but the guardian gets one more attack on Delvok before he gets away. Delvok nearly collapses when he realizes the DM rolled a 1 on the guardian's attack roll. With this critical miss, the stone ogre raises his boner club to swing but manages to accidentally impale the side of his head with it.

7: The Trap Stairs

Since Delvok is down to his last hit point, we decide to rest here. If Delvok rests for eight hours his spells will return and he'll be able to cast **Cure Light Wounds** again, as well as another **Sleep** spell.

The room is empty and seems to be safe. As long as we don't encounter a wandering monster, we should be fine. But knowing our Dungeon Master, he will surely allow us a peaceful rest. He likes to have as many players as possible in his game. He doesn't want Buzz Jepson's character to die.

While Delvok rests, Itaa, Loxi, and I sit in the corner of the room. Itaa leans against my side with her head on my shoulder. Her long green ears stretch all the way across my neck, tickling the other side of my chin.

"Ogre statues with boners?" Loxi says, with an annoyed face. "Is that supposed to be funny or something? Or sexy? Or cool? Or clever? What is wrong with these kids?"

"It's always been like that," I say. "Half the monsters I've fought usually have giant boners for no reason."

"The Dungeon Master is an immature little twat," she says.

I nod my head.

"And he's like our God," she says. "He created us and controls our whole existence."

"Completely," I say.

"I can't think of a worse God," she says.

"So you really think we can resist our players and the DM?" I ask.

"I hope so," she says. "No, I know so."

"How?"

"We should put it to the test," she says. "Whenever your player has you do something, just do the opposite."

"But what if the player is the person who is commanding me to do the opposite of what he says?"

"Then do the opposite of that," she says.

"But then I'd be doing what he originally wanted," I say.

"Look, there has to be a way," she says. "I'm not going to just give in and let somebody else control my life. I'm going to make decisions for myself."

"Like what?" I ask.

"For starters," she says. "I'm not going to try to kill you at the end of the quest and steal your gold. My alignment is neutral evil. That's what a character of neutral evil alignment would do. But I'm not going to act like a neutral evil character anymore. I don't give a shit what my character sheet says."

"But alignments can change," I say, "judging by the actions our players make for us. By the end of this quest your character sheet might have the alignment changed to true neutral or even neutral good, like me."

"More like chaotic good," she says. "At best. Of course, it's going to be hard being chaotic good with the class of assassin. I might need to change my class to thief, or fighter/thief."

"Or you can just retire as an adventurer," I say. "That's what I plan to do."

"Then what would you do if you weren't adventuring?" she asks.

"Pick up a trade. Find a wife. Raise a family."

"Sounds dull," she says.

"Exactly," I say.

When Delvok is fully rested, he casts **Cure Light Wounds** until he regains all of his hit points.

"Better?" I ask.

"Much better," he says.

But as we descend the staircase toward area 8, Delvok springs a trap. The staircase becomes a slide and we all go flying down the slope until we crash into the wall at the bottom of the stairs. This causes 1d6+1 points of damage.

Itaa is the luckiest, getting away with 2 points of damage. I lose 4. Loxi loses 3. And poor Delvok loses 5 hit points, bringing his total back down to 1.

Delvok is so infuriated by the events that he can't even speak.

"Your player must have really pissed off the Dungeon Master today," Loxi says.

"That would be illogical," Delvok says. "It was surely just bad luck."

But back in the real world, in the Donnelly home, Aaron is pissed off at Buzz Jepson and did purposely damage his player with both the trap and the ogre statue. He doesn't necessarily want to kill Delvok, but he is taking out his anger on Buzz's character because Buzz ate all the Cheetos.

8: Entrance to the Catacombs

I gather everyone together at the top of the stairs, to make a plan for the rest of the quest.

"Okay," I say. "From this point on, we do everything we can to resist our players. Don't do anything you would normally do."

"So you are saying," Delvok says, "the most logical move for us would be to act illogically?"

"Exactly," I say. "For starters, you should stop acting like a Vulcan."

Delvok frowns when I say that.

"Be emotional from now on," I say. "Say to hell with logic."

Delvok frowns.

"Go on, say it."

"To hell with logic," he says, quietly.

I smack him on the back (well, his hip) and say, "Now you're getting it." However, I can tell saying those words hurt him deeply.

I turn to Loxi, "And you try not to be such a sex-crazed slut."

"No problem," she says. "I'll only fuck 3 or 4 more people

through the rest of the quest."

"No, fuck nobody," I say.

Her facial expression joins Delvok's.

"And Itaa," I say to the goblin girl, in goblin tongue. "You stop talking like a cave man."

Itaa smiles.

"Yes!" she says. "Itaa speak normal now!"

"Well . . ." I say. "Not exactly. Try not speaking in third person. Refer to yourself as *I* from now on."

"Okay," Itaa says. "I Itaa speak normal now!"

I stare at her as her smile grows larger.

Then I say, "Close enough." I turn to the others. "And I will try to stop being a submissive coward. Let's all try to become our own people, our own characters. Let's reinvent ourselves."

They all nod their heads.

Then we take the staircase to the next level of the dungeon.

BACKSTAB

x2 to damage roll !

Aaron Donnely
Period 3

Algebra Notes

9/18/98

① $2x \cdot 3x = 6x^2$

$2x + 3x = 5x$

② $-4y \cdot y = -4y^2$

$-4y + y = -3y$

② $1\frac{1}{3} - \frac{3}{4}$

$1\frac{1}{3} = \frac{4}{12} + \frac{12}{12} = \frac{16}{12}$

$-\frac{3}{4} = \frac{9}{12} = -\frac{9}{12}$

$\frac{7}{12}$

orc

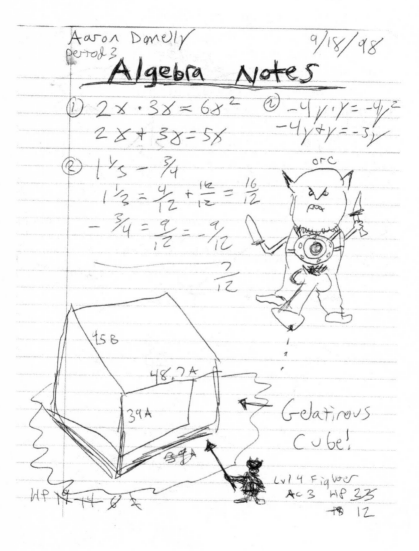

45B

48.7A

39A

39A

HP 14 14 8 2

Gelatinous
Cube!

Lvl 4 Fighter
Ac 3 HP 33
tb 12

hoopak

2 hand sword

Mancatcher

$\frac{1}{3} - \frac{3}{4}$

$\frac{4}{3} - \frac{3}{4}$

$\frac{16}{12} - \frac{9}{12}$

$\frac{2}{2}$

d4

d6

d8

$\frac{1}{3}$

$\frac{-1}{} - \frac{3}{4}$

$\frac{7}{12}$

$\frac{1}{3} \cdot \frac{-3}{4}$

$\frac{4}{3} \cdot \frac{-3}{4} = -1$

my Elf
girlfriend

Penis Gauntlet

Wed 9/23/98   Notes

p 527 #9 to #19

Properties to Justify   Arrow
statements   Damage!!

Associative Property
    for +
    for ×

$(2+3)+4 = 2+(3+4)$

$(2\cdot3)\cdot4 = 2\cdot(3\cdot4)$

↑ group changing

$\frac{6}{2}$ binary operation

Woooo!

Commutative Property
    for +
    for ×

ex:

$3+4 = 4+$

Purple worm

Halfling

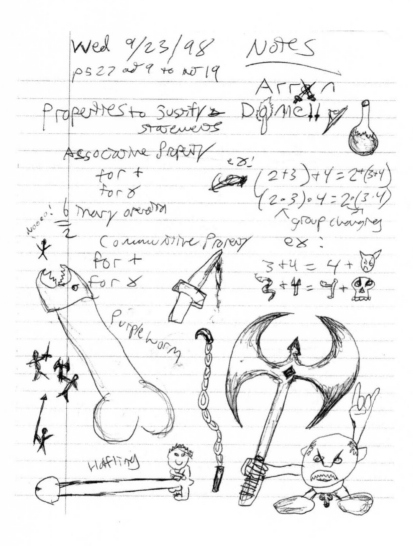

⑥ Show $X^2 - 3$ in different ups

40   44/84 $x+x+4=100$
48+4   55/100 $2x+4=100$

Inverse Props
5 + 0 = 5
5 · 1 = 5
for + added waves = 5 + 5 = 0 destroy
5 · $\frac{1}{5}$ = $\frac{5}{5}$!

Vaginas by Race

boring → human

Elf — No pubic hair

Gnome — landing strip

locks → Dwarf

half-orc — pierced, tiny

Halfling

stripe tattoos → Goblin

Kobold — scales, hair

Gnoll

$$a = -6x^3 + 2 \quad ; \; x = -1$$
$$a = -6(-1)^3 + 2$$
$$a = -6(-1) + 2 = 6 + 2 = \boxed{8}$$

D and fucking D !

Beholder

Displacer Beast

DW Slime

ancient catacombs

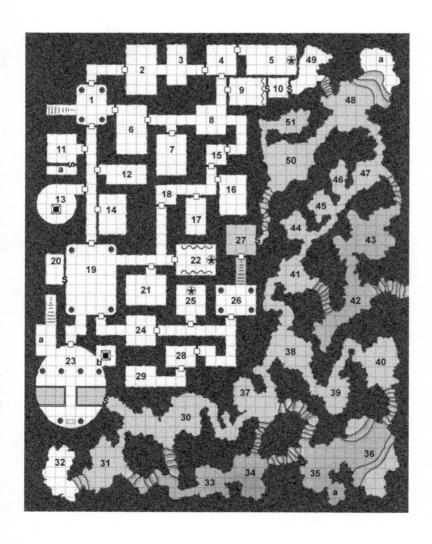

1: Tennant Temple

We arrive in a large temple, which was once used by Lord Tennant to worship the Gods of Time. There are four large columns in this room, each one painted with a different god: a crazy-eyed man with a long striped scarf, a man with frizzy blond hair and a motley colored coat, a short man with an umbrella cane that has a question mark handle, and a young man with blond hair wearing a cricket jumper with question marks on his lapels. In the center of the room is the object of worship: a blue phone box.

As we cross the room toward the eastern door, we encounter a **rust monster (AC 2, HD 5, hp 27, ATK 2, DMG nil, SA cause rust)**. When it sees us, it charges for Loxi.

"This is highly illogical," Delvok says. "According to the Monster Manual, a rust monster will never attack unprovoked."

"What did I say about logic, Delvok?" I say.

Loxi points her sword at the creature. "Well, it looks like it is attacking anyway."

Then she swings her broad sword at it.

"Don't use your sword," I cry. "It'll rust it!"

When the rust monster attacks her broad sword, the metal blade twists and reddens. However, it doesn't rust. Instead, the blade of the sword mutates into a dildo.

Loxi examines the dildo sword. "What the hell?"

"It did not rust the blade," Delvok says. "But it did render it useless."

The rust monster goes for Loxi's other sword, but she backs off.

I realize that the rust monster is actually a **dildo monster (AC 2, HD 5, hp 27, ATK 2, DMG nil, SA cause dildo)**.

"This is just getting stupid," Loxi says, as the little beetle-like critter crawls after her.

I nod my head. "Yeah, it's about 3:30am in the real world right now. The players are probably getting bored and delirious from staying up all night."

The dildo monster jumps at her other blade, but she rolls a successful dexterity score check and dodges out of the way.

"Let's get out of here," she says.

We all agree.

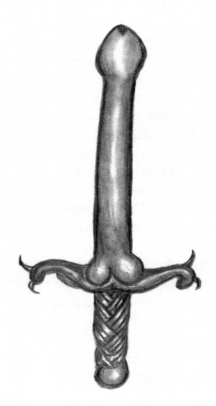

dildo sword +1 (+3 vs hobgoblins)

6: Metal Room

After entering this room, I am completely sure our players are getting bored in the real world right now. In this room, a stereo is blasting death metal music from speakers that reach to the top of the ceiling. Thirty-two **orcs (AC: 6, HD 1, hp 5, 5, 5, 5, 5, 6, 6, 7, 7, 7, 7, 7, 7, 7, 8, 8, 9, 9, 9, 10, 11, 11, 11, 11, 12, 12, 13, 13, 13, 13, 14 #AT 1, D 1-6)** are in the middle of the room, slam-dancing in an enormous mosh pit. Most of them wear blue jeans and leather jackets, with concert t-shirts from old death metal bands like Deicide and Cannibal Corpse. They have piercings, upside-down cross tattoos, and combat boots.

The only way to get across the room will be to go through the mosh pit.

"Ready?" I yell, over the music.

The others nod while covering their ears.

Then we enter the mosh pit. I can hear d20s rolling in the real world as we receive strength and dexterity checks. Orcs slam us with their shoulders on all sides and we try to keep ourselves upright. It's a little known fact, but orcs are the best race when it comes to moshing.

I lose a dexterity roll and an orc slams me so hard I lose a hit point.

"Shit!" I yell at the others. "These orcs can cause damage with their mosh attacks. If Delvok gets hit he's going to die."

We decide to put Delvok in the middle of us so that we get all the damage from the mosh pit. The death metal orcs continue their assault, slamming us on all sides. I lose a few more hit points, Loxi and Itaa also lose one.

I have to hold Itaa tightly by the arm. Because we're so small we might get carried away within the pit. When I look

up at Loxi she has a frustrated look on her face.

"What's wrong?" I yell up at her.

"I'm resisting the DM," she says. "He wants me to mosh."

"Don't do it!" I say.

"It's hard to resist," she says. "I'm a punk rock elf."

Then she attacks one of the orcs with her dildo sword, smacking it in his face like a morning star, causing him to lose two hit points.

"Try as hard as you can," I say.

We get to the other side with only losing a few more hit points each. Delvok is lucky to get out of there alive. Once we're out in the hall, we lean against the walls and catch our breaths.

Itaa smiles up at me.

"Itaa like mosh," she says.

I pat her on the head.

7: Sex Dungeon

This room is designed like sex dungeons found in the real world. Chains, torture racks, bondage gear, sex swings, and leather straps fill the room. On the side of the wall there is a weapon rack, only instead of weapons it is filled with dildos, flogs, and other assorted sex toys.

In the center of the room is a naked **orc female sex slave (AC: 8, HD 1, hp 6, #AT 1, D 1-2)** tied to a rack. She has a voluptuous figure, greenish-gray skin, large breasts, bulldog-like teeth pointing up from her bottom lip, and two black pigtails sticking out of a bald head. Like many female monsters in this world, she is a lot sexier than how you'd think an orc would look. According to our Dungeon Master, all fantasy creatures are fuckable.

She wiggles and squirms in her bondage gear as we enter,

eyeing us and moaning, as if she's begging us to fuck her.

"Anyone want to have sex with an orc?" Loxi asks.

"Not really," I say.

And so we leave.

8: Corridor

The players and Dungeon Master in the real world are beginning to wonder why we aren't doing what they want us to do. We didn't allow the dildo monster to turn our weapons into dildos and then use the dildos on each other. They also probably wanted us to run around the rest of the game killing things with big dildo swords. Then we didn't mosh with the orcs. Now we didn't have sex with the orc girl in the sex dungeon.

"It's working," Loxi says. "I think we're really resisting them."

My character seems sad and disappointed with his role playing. He really wanted me to mosh in the last room.

"Let's try not to piss them off too much," I say. "Even if we're able to do whatever we want to do the Dungeon Master still has control of this world. He can throw pretty much anything at us if he wants us dead."

The others agree. For all we know, the DM might throw a goddamned tarrasque at us in the next room.

15: Fountain of Healing

In the middle of this room, there is a shallow pool. In the center of the pool is a statue of a pixie with eight boobs spraying water out of its nipples. When we drink from the fountain, all of our wounds are healed.

"That's pretty convenient," I say, as all of my hit points return.

"Yes." Delvok nods, then counts all 6 of his hit points in his body to make sure they are all there. "Satisfactory."

16: Porno Room

In this room, there are dozens of televisions running along all four walls. Each television is screening Japanese hentai porn films. The room is filled with the cartoonish sounds of Japanese anime characters having sex, most of which involve tentacle monsters raping busty bunny women. In the center of the room, a **beholder (AC 0/2/7, HD 11, hp 75, #AT 1, DMG 2-8, SA magic spell like attacks)** is watching all of the hentai films at the same time, with each of his many eyes facing every television screen at once.

His large mouth is wide open, his fat tongue hanging out, floating three feet above the ground as he watches the porn films. It is a little known fact that beholders are all addicted to watching hentai. Even though they do not have sex organs and therefore can not masturbate, it is still the biggest weakness of the beholder. When watching these animated porn films, they are unable to attack or defend themselves.

We could enter the room and kill the beholder right now and it would not fight back. It would be an easy way to gain a lot of experience points and maybe go up a level or two. But it is what the players want us to do, so we decide to move on instead.

17: Dice Room

When we enter this room, we realize that the Dungeon Master really doesn't give a fuck about anything anymore. He's just trying to make his friends laugh. He doesn't give a crap if we all die and they start a new game with new characters next week. Because this is just plain stupid.

In the center of the room is the biggest, dumbest, most retarded creature Aaron Donnelly has ever invented for a Dungeons and Dragons module. It is a **d20 with boobs (AC 1, HD 5, hp 36, #Att 1, DMG 1d10).** Yeah, that's right, bouncing up and down in the middle of the room is a giant 20-sided die with enormous humanoid breasts on its 18th side.

When it sees us, it rolls at us. The thing mows us down like a bowling ball hitting pins and we each lose 4 hit points. I try attacking it, but its armor class is too good.

"Let's just get out of here," I say, shaking my head.

The thing attacks me. Because it is a d20, the monster rolls itself for its attack rolls. However, since it can control its own movements it can always land on 20 with every single roll. So it attacks me, rolls a 20, a critical hit, and does double damage, taking off 14 of my hit points.

Before it can attack again, we get the hell out of here. Then we go back to the fountain to get all of our hit points back.

ẟ20

with boobs

18: Figure Room

In this room, there are a bunch of giant pewter figures. I'm guessing the Dungeon Master has gotten so bored he is putting dice and pewter figures on top of the map in the middle of the table, telling the players they are actually monsters their characters have to fight.

The pewter figures come alive and try to kill us. We yawn and leave the room. The only interesting thing about them is that one of them is actually the pewter figurine that Todd used to represent The Dwarf Lord.

22: Orgy Room

When we enter this room, we walk right into the middle of a massive gnoll orgy. We find **Gnoryc, the Gnoll King (AC: 3, MV 9", HD 2, hp 35 #AT 1, D: two-handed sword, 1-10)** and nine of his **gnoll marauders (AC: 5, MV 9", HD 2, hp 15, 15, 14, 14, 14, 13, 13, 11, 11 #AT 1, D: 1-10)** in the midst of a hardcore fucking session.

Before we can sneak back out the way we came in, we are spotted.

"Look at who came to join us," Gnoryc says, in gnollish. All the gnolls stop fucking and turn to us. "Four adventurers have decided to volunteer themselves as sex slaves for our daily orgy party." His voice is high and feminine. He also speaks gnollish with a British accent.

The gnolls grab us and bring us into the room. There are

four males and five females. The tall naked hyena creatures stare down on us with hungry faces and massive hard-ons.

"The Dungeon Master's catching on to us," I say. "If we're not going to volunteer to engage in sex then he's going to force it onto us."

Delvok nods at me as a large gnoll forces him to his knees. "Even if we control our own actions, the Dungeon Master will always control the world around us. He can bend our reality around until we submit to his will."

Gnoryc reclines in a pink chaise lounge, rubbing his massive furry schlong through sheer pantyhose. Aside from the pantyhose, he wears nothing but a white rose that is perched behind an ear. Two of his underlings, one male and one female, massage his royal naked body.

"Divvy them up amongst yourselves, my friends," says the Gnoll King. "Have your way with them as you wish, but try not to damage them too much. We can always reuse them for our sex dungeon."

The gnolls cackle and howl at us. The gnolls who want us come for us. The male gnoll who has Delvok on the ground chooses him, and takes him aside. Two male gnolls choose Loxi, planning to share her at the same time. A large male gnoll grabs Itaa and throws her over his shoulder.

She reaches out for me, crying, "Halfman! Save Itaa!" as she is taken away.

A female gnoll chooses me. I look up at her. She is so tall that the top of my head doesn't even reach her vagina. She looks down on me with a snarling hyena face. Then takes me to her bed. Next to me, the two male gnolls have already gotten to work on Loxi. They have pulled her clothes off and sandwiched her between them, raping her from both orifices. Judging by the look of shock and agony on her face, she has never had sex with two penises at the same time, let alone giant hairy gnoll dicks. She tries to resist them, but their strength scores are just too high for her. Now she kind of knows how I felt when she and Juzii had their way with me. An elf with two gnolls is about the same as a halfling with two elves. It is impossible for her to overpower them.

But that is an unfair comparison. Outside of getting the STD, I kind of enjoyed having sex with the two elf girls. Loxi, on the other hand, is not enjoying being raped by these two animal men. I realize that Aaron Donnelly must have a huge furry fetish. Otherwise, I don't know why he would want us to be forced into an orgy with hyena people. Or maybe he just thinks it's funny.

I can't see where they have taken Itaa, but Delvok is nearby. Before he can be anally penetrated by another large penis—his ass is probably still sore from taking Juzii's harpy dick not too long ago—he casts **Sleep** on the gnoll. The hyena man falls asleep on top of him. Delvok looks around to make sure nobody notices, then he creates mock-humping motions against the sleeping gnoll's crotch so that the others

think they are doing it.

As the gnoll woman strips me of my clothing, her claw so large it can cover my entire chest, I sneak the Dildo of Enlightenment +2 out of my Bag of Holding. Once the gnoll straddles me and tries to drop her vagina onto my penis, I position the dildo in my crotch so that she fucks it instead.

She doesn't realize it's not my dick at first. I hold it in place as she fucks it, smothering my entire body with her furry stomach. Once she realizes that the dildo doesn't feel right, she pulls up and looks down at my crotch. At first, she's surprised to see the dildo. But then the dildo's magic seeps in. She freezes on top of me as the knowledge of her true existence seeps into her head.

In gnollish, she tells me, "Not possible. I can't just be an imaginary character created to satisfy a fat crippled kid's furry fetish."

"I'm sorry," I tell her. "I had to do it. I need your help."

"What do you want from me?" she asks.

"Get us out of here," I say. "You know the truth now. You know that we're being controlled by kids from another world."

The Gnoll King and a few other gnolls notice that we are just talking and aren't having sex. They give her a dirty look until panic crosses her face. She nods at them and then grabs my real penis.

"What are you doing?" I ask her, as she strokes me with two fingers to give me an erection.

"The king gets angry if we don't have sex," she says. "We don't have a choice."

"Just pretend we're fucking," I tell her.

But she puts me inside of her anyway, then starts fucking me. But since our size difference is so vast, I don't really feel much of anything but wetness. I don't think she feels much of anything either. So we continue our conversation.

"You can resist," I tell her. "That's what the four of us

are trying to do. We want to resist our players, resist the Dungeon Master, and be our own characters."

She shakes her head, and keeps fucking me.

"No," she says. "We should just do what we're supposed to do. Just try to ignore the knowledge and pretend like it's not true."

"No, we can't do that," I say. "That's what the Dungeon Master wants us to do. He wants us to be compliant, and have sex with each other in strange horrific ways to fulfill his nerdy little fantasies."

She closes her eyes and shuts me out. Then she moans and then fucks me faster. She seems to have already made up her mind. She's on the Dungeon Master's side. She's an obedient NPC, a weak conformist, even with the dildo's knowledge. But then I conform with her. She has found a way to get sensation out of my tiny penis by rubbing it against her clitoris. I feel it, too. I let myself ejaculate prematurely, cumming in her fur. Then my penis goes limp and she's not able to have sex with me anymore. Now, hopefully, she'll listen.

"Look," I say. "You should join us. Help us figure out a way to resist the Dungeon Master."

"Now you're going to have to lick me until I have an orgasm," she says.

"No, you need to listen to me."

"I don't want to hear about it," she says. "Now shut up and lick my pussy or I will smother you to death with it."

"I will if you just hear me out for a second," I say.

She groans at me and sneezes hyena snot all over my chest.

"Hurry," she says.

"You'd be better off joining us," I say. "Since we're the player characters, the world pretty much revolves around us. For all you know, by the time we leave this room you might no longer exist."

"I existed before you came into this room," she says.

"Are you sure?" I say. "What if you were only just born

the minute we walked through that door? What if all of your past memories were implanted into your brain in the same instant that we arrived? Your whole life has been fabricated by the Dungeon Master for the sole purpose of fucking me right at this moment. Once you're no longer relevant to our quest you'll just disappear. Maybe you won't die, but your existence will be put on hold forever."

"You're making my head hurt," she says. "Can't you just make me cum? It would be a lot easier if we just did it that way."

"Are you sure you want to live the rest of your life as a puppet?" I ask.

She takes a moment to think about it.

"No," she says. "But what are we going to do? What *can* we do?"

People notice we're not fucking again and so she starts humping my stomach.

"I don't know," I say. "Maybe you can get the king to let us go."

"I am a loyal subject of my king," she says. "I could ask but I don't know how I could persuade him. Like myself, he was invented by a horny teenager. All he thinks about is sex. It's not likely that he would give up his sex slaves for anything or anyone."

"Well, maybe you can ask to do all four of us at the same time," I say. "Situate us near the door. Then we can all escape with ease."

"My brothers and sisters would never let me hog all of the sex slaves to myself," she says. "We share everything. In fact, I probably won't be able to fuck you for much longer before I have to pass you off to the next gnoll."

"There's got to be something you can do," I say.

She thinks about it for a minute while humping my stomach. The weight of her crotch on my midsection is beginning to bruise my internal organs.

170

"I think I know what to do," she says. "Come with me."

She takes me to the Gnoll King.

"Ah, Mirrin," says Gnoryc, stretching his pantyhose up past his bellybutton. "Have you brought me a present?"

She hesitates to speak, afraid to tell him no.

He says, "A halfling would look good on the end of my royal cock, wouldn't you say?"

"Yes, sire," she says.

She pauses.

Before he can grab me, she says, "But I have an idea for what to do with him."

The Gnoll King expresses annoyance at her words.

"Speak," he says.

"What if we were to bring these four slaves to the wizard Olffgel?" she says.

"Olffgel!" he cries. "I have given that twatty gnome more than enough of my sex slaves. He has no need for these."

"N-no," she says. "I mean . . . What if we had the wizard cast an enchantment on them? One that would cause them to magically grow dicks and vaginas all over their bodies. Then we can gangbang each of them all at the same time."

The king taps his finger against the side of his muzzle, thinking about it. I can't tell, but it seems as if he's suspicious of the suggestion.

"Does he have such a magic spell?" he asks.

"Yes," she says. "It's a new one. He discovered it only recently."

"Are you sure?" he asks.

"Positive," she says.

The king's face lights up. "Splendid! Why don't you and Toryc take these slaves to the wizard. Don't return them until they are covered with new holes and appendages."

"Yes, sire," she says, turning us away from him.

"And Mirrin," he says. She turns back. "If you happen to be wrong about this spell know that we will still be gangbanging somebody all at the same time. But it won't be one of these slaves, it will be you. And instead of using magic to give you multiple vaginas we'll do it the old fashion way." Then his smile turns into a frown. "We'll cut them into you with our swords. A dozen of them. All over your body."

A look of shock crosses Mirrin's face.

"Yes, sire," she says.

Then she walks me away from him.

She mumbles loudly at me, "I can't believe I let you talk me into this. You're going to get me killed."

I give her the thumbs up. Then I look for my friends. Delvok is still hiding under the sleeping gnoll. The two male gnolls toss Loxi aside once they're done with her. Her entire torso is covered with their sperm, concentrated near her vagina which seems to still be oozing out of her in a thick stream. They must have ejaculated at least two pints of the stuff, each.

When I help Loxi off the ground, she sighs deeply with exhaustion.

"Are you okay?" I ask.

She takes another deep breath as she wipes large handfuls of hyena gunk off of her boobs.

Then she says, "That was awesome."

"What? Are you serious?"

"Oh man," she says. "I haven't been fucked like that in a long time."

"I thought you were in pain."

"Yeah, it was great."

"I thought you weren't going to be a dirty slut anymore?" I ask.

"Given the choice," she says, "I wouldn't volunteer for anything like that again, but I was created to love that kind of shit. It was nothing short of awesome."

I shake my head at her, completely disappointed.

Mirrin retrieves the gnoll Toryc who was ordered to help

bring us to the wizard. Toryc, by coincidence, is the same gnoll who was trying to fuck Delvok. He has a confused look on his face when Mirrin wakes him up. He doesn't realize Delvok cast **Sleep** on him and figures he just fell asleep on the elf just before sex.

I scan the room for Itaa. A 3' goblin girl is hard to find among all the hairy giant gnolls. Then I spot her on the other side of the room. She is naked and squirming at the mercy of a particularly large male gnoll. She hisses, spits, and growls loudly at the hyena man, kicking and punching. This whole time, he has been trying to get his penis inside of her but she squirms too much and her vagina is just way too small for his size. He tries lubing up her vagina with his hyena tongue, but it's not enough. Whenever he puts his face too close to her she pokes him in the eye with her thin pointy finger.

As I go through the crowd of humping hyenas to get to her, I see the look of frustration on the gnoll's face. Since he can't get his dick inside of her vagina, he tries to put it in her mouth. Not a good idea. Before I can get to Itaa, the gnoll tells Itaa to open her mouth and points his dick at her throat. It's too late. Itaa opens her mouth alright, but only to bite down as hard she can on the end of his penis.

The gnolls yelps and screams. He jumps to his feet, but Itaa still has his dick between her sharp needle-like teeth, growling at it. The gnoll thrashes Itaa around, trying to shake her off of his dick, but she won't let go.

"Itaa!" I say, as I get to them.

But she confuses what I mean by the word. Instead of thinking I just called her name, she thinks I said *attack!* and bites down even harder. The gnoll's shriek becomes high-pitched.

"Itaa, let him go," I say.

Itaa's yellow eyes look over at me. Then she opens her mouth and drops to the floor. She runs over to me and hides behind my back, hugging me close to her.

"Itaa hate licky gnoll," she says.

The gnoll is furious at her. He looks at the two of us as if he is going to rip our throats out. The Gnoll King recognizes his subject's discontent and decides to appease him.

"Mirrin," Gnoryc says to the gnoll woman, "make sure Olffgel puts a vagina on this goblin's forehead, right between her eyes." He turns to his angry subject. "Then you will have the pleasure of fucking her brains out, quite literally."

This calms the gnoll's aggression. His snarl then turns into a wicked smile. He cackles at the goblin and points at her.

He says, "By the end of the day I'll be picking your ugly goblinoid brains out of my foreskin."

But Itaa has no idea what he just said.

Mirrin hands us our belongings and pulls us away from the other gnolls. After we get dressed, Toryc and Mirrin escort us out of the room to go meet the gnome wizard, Olffgel Zookwar.

21: Wizard's Chamber

When we arrive in the great wizard's chamber, we run into two large dragons, one gold and one blue. Well, they aren't exactly dragons. They are giant dragonoid creatures, ones that don't actually exist in any edition of the Monster Manual. The dragonoids have the bodies of voluptuous human females. They have the shapely figures of women, with large breasts and curvy hips, but they have the scales, claws, tails, and heads of dragons. They also have long flowing hair (the blue dragon's hair is golden, the gold dragon's hair is light blue) that glitters in the torchlight. Their pubic hair is also glittery. The two giant dragonoids are in the middle of having hardcore lesbian sex. They are putting on a show for their master.

Olffgel Zookwar, the gnome wizard, is lying naked in a cushy chair, masturbating to the lesbian dragon sex. He is a little man, even for a gnome, with a bald head, a small gray child-molester mustache, and perky pink nipples that are a little too long for a male.

The chair in which he's sitting is made of asses. It is a collection of over a dozen buttocks from women of many different races, all sewn together to form a comfortable fleshy piece of furniture. There are brown human butts, green orc butts, furry gnoll butts, white hobgoblin butts, little pixie butts, shiny dark elf butts, and a giant ogre butt as the back rest. The asses seem to wiggle and twitch all around Olffgel, as if the flesh is still living. Each pair of butt cheeks seem to have a life of its own.

He caresses a quickling butt with his left hand as he jerks himself off with his right. When Mirrin approaches him he gives her the evil eye, not wanting to be interrupted until after he is finished. Mirrin holds us back, completely terrified of the man who is a third her size.

While the dragonoids finger each other, licking their breasts with long forked tongues, I notice something odd about the creatures. I don't think they are actually real. I believe they are actually just an illusion created by Olffgel. Perhaps he creates illusions that he can masturbate to like pornography.

When he finishes, Olffgel squirts his spunk onto a pair of dwarf butt cheeks. Then he stands up, pulls up his tiny silver speedos, and walks over to us. Behind him, a small tongue emerges from between the dwarf butt cheeks and licks the cum off of itself. It makes hungry slurping noises as it swallows. Then it burps.

"What can I do for Gnoryc this time?" asks the gnome. "As you can see, I have work to do."

I can tell Mirrin is afraid to tell him the truth. If Olffgel actually did have the ability to put multiple sex organs on us she probably would have had the wizard do that to us

instead, so that she could go back to serving the Gnoll King and continue life accepting the fact that she's just a pawn of the Dungeon Master.

"We have something to show you," Mirrin says.

We go to a table cluttered with scrolls and potions. She takes my Bag of Holding from me and removes the Dildo of Enlightenment +2. Behind us, the dragonoids are still engaging in fierce tongue-fucking.

"This dildo possesses powerful magic," she tells him, and backs away so that he can investigate it for himself.

His eyes widen at the thought of a magical dildo. He goes to his table, licking his lips excitedly as he examines it.

"There is definitely magic in this," he says, smiling. "What does it do? Does it cause the user to have one million orgasms all at the same time? Does it come to life and fuck you all on its own, hands-free? Does its size grow and shift so that it fits perfectly in the user's vagina?"

Mirrin shakes her head. "No, it's a different kind of magic dildo. When it is used, it gives you secret knowledge of the universe."

"Secret knowledge?"

"Yes," she says. "I have used it. So have these four prisoners."

Then he rolls his eyes and steps away from the table.

"Why would I have a use for such an item?" he says. "A dildo with non-sexual magic is of no value to me. You're wasting my time."

He turns toward the dragon women and watches them lick each other's pubic regions, huffing and snorting in pleasure.

"But this is knowledge you really should know," she says. "It will change the way you view the world."

"I like my view of the world just fine," he says.

I step forward and say, "We could really use your help. You are a wise and powerful wizard. With you on our side I'm sure we could figure a way out of this."

Perhaps he even has a spell that could transport us from this world into the real world, so that we can live the rest of our lives as real beings rather than imaginary ones. Of course, it might be odd for people in the real world to see elves, halflings, gnolls, gnomes, and goblins walking around, but I'd rather be real and out of place than imaginary and at the mercy of a Dungeon Master.

"I'm not going to use it and that's final," he says. "I will never use it. Now, I'm a very busy man and must get back to my business. If you do not leave this instant I will just have to include the lot of you in my work."

Damn. I know what's going on. Aaron Donnelly is in control of Olffgel Zookwar. He isn't going to let any more NPCs use the dildo, because every time they do he loses control of them and then they join our side. He doesn't want Olffgel to join us, too. Olffgel is his most powerful NPC.

"Fine," Mirrin says, grabbing the dildo.

"Wait," he says. "Leave that." He points at the dildo. "I will find a use for it. Perhaps it would be good for trade at the magic-user's sex shop."

He holds out his hand to take it. Mirrin obeys and hands it over to him. The coward.

"Wait a fucking minute!" Loxi cries. She isn't going to let him get away with it. "That's ours. Give it back."

The gnome chuckles. "This was yours? Oh, too bad. It's mine now."

Loxi draws her sword and attacks the gnome. Without wearing any protective armor, the gnome is easy to hit in an attack roll. She stabs him in the shoulder and does four points of damage. Not enough to faze him.

"That's it!" Olffgel says. "You have all just volunteered yourselves for my experiments in sexual sorcery!" He looks at the gnoll female. "Including you, Mirrin."

Mirrin kneels at the wizard, totally submitting to his command. Loxi sneers at her for being so compliant. She would never give in so easily.

Loxi slashes at Olffgel again, this time grazing the side of his head for 7 points of damage. He roars with anger at the woman.

"You will pay for that!" says the wizard.

Then the giant dragonoids turn to us. The gold one grabs Loxi and picks her up off the ground in its massive claws. Loxi struggles to free herself as the dragonoid shoves her between its massive 10' wide breasts. (DM NOTE: Each breast takes up a square on the dungeon map). She slashes at the dragon, but its scales are too tough for her blade.

"Now you will feed the sexual hunger of my dragon girls," he yells.

The blue dragon woman scoops Delvok and Mirrin from the floor and licks them with its long tongue. Its mouth is so large that it could swallow them both whole in a single gulp. When Toryc sees this, he believes the dragonoid is actually eating them, rather than attempting to give them oral pleasure. Not wanting to be next on the menu, he panics and runs for the door.

"No one escapes!" the wizard yells.

Then the gold dragon girl holding Loxi in her breasts stomps her foot down on the gnoll man. He collapses to the floor, losing 10 hit points. In the next round, the dragon's scaly foot presses harder on the gnoll's body until he's crushed to death. The dragon foot grinds his corpse into the floor like a furry cockroach.

Itaa hides behind my back, wrapping her arms around me frantically, as if nothing bad could happen to her if she just squeezes me tighter.

The gold dragon girl bends down for us, and picks us off the ground. Itaa screams in panic, clawing at my neck and shoulders, taking a hit point from me and leaving large red gashes, without knowing what she's doing. But the dragon isn't actually the thing holding me off the ground, it is Itaa.

The dragonoid can't actually do anything to me. It can't pick me up. It can't put me in its breasts. It can't squash me with its foot. This is because the dragonoids are just an illusion, as I figured out upon our arrival in the Wizard's Chamber.

When I slip out of Itaa's grasp, I drop to the ground, losing another hit point in the fall. The dragonoid tries to pick me up again, but her scaly hand just passes through me.

The gnome wizard comes to my side. At first, I think he's going to cast an attack spell on me for being impervious to his illusion. But he just stands next to me, casually. He picks up a gnome-sized bong from the floor and smokes a bowl.

"So it doesn't work on you, huh?" he says, as he holds in

the smoke. "That's too bad."

He exhales and passes me the bong. I take it, so as not to be rude. I couldn't take on a 7th level wizard single-handedly, even if he's naked and unarmed, so I'll try to stay on his good side.

"They are the lucky ones," he says. "Since they think it's all real they actually can have sex with anything I create for them. But for you and I, we know they are illusions so they won't work on us. You have to believe for them to be real."

The dragon girls lie down and make out with each other. They put all four humanoids between their four breasts like they're in some kind of boob-cage and then squeeze each other's breasts against their squirming bodies. As the dragons kiss, the blue one licks Itaa up into its mouth and then sucks on her like a piece of hard candy. They pass her little hissing green body back and forth between their mouths as they french kiss.

Then the gold dragon takes Delvok and puts him halfway inside the blue dragon's vagina. Then she takes Mirrin and shoves her inside of the blue dragon's asshole. The elf and gnoll scream as they see the gold dragon's blue pubic hair coming toward them. The top halves of Delvok and Mirrin disappear into the vagina and anus of the other dragon. Then the dragons fuck each other, using the elf and the gnoll as living double-dildos. I can hear their muffled screams.

"Nice," Olffgel says as he sees Mirrin going in and out of his dragon girls' assholes.

Because he thinks this is all real, Delvok begins to asphyxiate within the dragon's golden vagina. He also loses a hit point every round due to the pressure of the tightening vaginal muscles. If he doesn't get out of there soon he is going to die.

I hand the bong back to the wizard. As he goes to take a hit, I yell up at Delvok.

"It's just an illusion!" I yell at him. "If you don't believe in it nothing will happen to you!"

Delvok hears me. His saving throw roll is successful and the illusion breaks its hold on him. He slips out of the blue dragon's body and lands on the floor. Loxi, too, overhears us, and breaks the illusion. Itaa and Mirrin, unfortunately, fail their saving throws. They don't have the intelligence to tell the difference between illusion and reality.

When Loxi hits the ground, she charges the wizard with her broad sword. He casts **Web** on her and she becomes entangled in sticky string, holding her in place. I draw my short sword +1 and stab the wizard, taking off a few hit points. He looks at me with surprise, as if he didn't expect me to turn on him. As if sharing a bowl together was more than enough to create a bond of friendship.

Delvok attacks him with his long sword, cutting him across the chest for 2 points of damage. Then Olffgel cries out as he uses his bong as a weapon. He smashes it across Delvok's face. The DM rolls a 20, critical hit, so the glass shatters and cuts Delvok's throat open, killing him instantly.

But before Delvok's lifeless corpse hits the floor, time rewinds itself. His throat heals up and the bong puts itself back together, as if the attack had never happened. Delvok, Olffgel, and I stare at each other, confused about what had just happened.

"What the fuck was that?" I say.

Delvok feels his throat.

He says, "It appears my player demanded a re-roll because the dice had fallen on the floor. The Dungeon Master complied. So instead of a 20, Olffgel's new attack roll ended up being 5. A miss."

Olffgel has no idea what we're talking about. He just shakes his head in disbelief. Then we continue the fight. I attack with a hit, but Delvok misses. Then Olffgel casts **Sleep** on us, but we are able to resist the spell. We attack again, and bring him down to his last few hit points.

To escape death, Olffgel casts **Invisibility** and runs away. Loxi breaks free of the **Web** spell and looks around the room for him. She swings her sword at random, hoping to land a lucky hit.

Behind us, the dragon girls continue their lesbian foursome with Mirrin and Itaa. However, Mirrin has long since expired within the gold dragon's asshole. I'm not sure if she was crushed to death or if she suffocated, but she's dead none the less. Itaa is still alive and well, though, biting furiously on a blue dragon nipple. She thinks she is causing it pain, but the dragon reacts to her as if it is pleasure.

We listen for the sounds of Olffgel's footsteps, but the dragons are so loud that we can't hear anything.

"Guard the door," Loxi tells me.

I nod and run for the door, waving my short sword +1 around as I go. But before I get there, the door opens up on its own.

"He's escaping!" I say.

But it's not an invisible figure opening the door from within. No, somebody is entering from the outside. My face drops in shock as we see him enter. The little reptilian figure casually steps inside. Then the kobold gives me a wide smile as he recognizes me.

"There you are," Glimworm says. "I've been looking for you everywhere."

The kobold wizard raises his hand at me, a sparkling of red magical energy builds up at his fingertips. I hold up my hands to block my face, but then realize he's not aiming for me. He casts **Magic Missile** at the invisible figure behind me. Olffgel Zookwar's invisibility spell dissipates and his corpse hits the ground.

Then the lesbian dragon illusion fades and Itaa finds herself lying on the floor next to Mirrin's fluffy dead body. She rubs her head, completely confused about what had just happened.

"You never returned my dildo," Glimworm tells me.

I fall on my knees and beg him for mercy. Delvok joins

me on the floor, but Loxi stays on her feet with her sword at the ready.

"Please," I say. "Don't kill us."

"Kill you?" he asks, with a confused face.

"It wasn't our fault," I tell him. "We didn't want to use the dildo, but these she-trolls raped us with it."

"It was beyond our control," Delvok says.

Glimworm stares at us, rubbing his chin. Then he laughs.

"I'm not going to kill you," he says, pulling me to my feet. "I guess I should have used a less threatening tactic to keep you from using the item."

Delvok and I look at each other, then nearly collapse with relief.

"I only said that to persuade you against using the dildo," he says. "As you know, the knowledge you have gained is knowledge you would be better off not knowing."

He looks at Loxi and then Itaa. "All four of you have used it, I see. That's too bad, but perhaps now that you understand the truth of this universe you might be willing to help me."

We listen.

"I have a plan to fix our situation," he says. "With your help, I believe we can be free of our makers by the end of the day."

"What do you have in mind?" Loxi asks.

"All in good time, elf," the kobold says. "All in good time."

He holds out his hand. "The dildo, please." Delvok runs to the table and retrieves it for him. Once in his hand, Glimworm sniffs the dildo twice and cringes at the odor. Then he wipes it against his robe and sniffs again.

"Come with me," he says. "We have much to discuss."

Then he leads us out of the room into the hallway.

19: Inner Sanctum

We stroll through a great hallway toward area 23. The Dungeon Master throws a gang of bugbears at us, but Glimworm casts **Sleep** and they all drop to the ground.

"There is a magical device in the next room that will suit our needs," says the kobold. "It is the one thing in this world that can ensure our permanent freedom from the gods."

"Will the players never be able to control us again?" Delvok asks.

"The players are our gods," says Glimworm. "But you know as well as I that these gods are flawed. This is true of all gods, including the god our players worship. They are average beings with strengths, weaknesses, doubts, confusion, apprehension, mercy, cruelty. They are just like us. The only thing that makes them gods is that they have dominion over another world."

"Don't tell me they're just like us," Loxi says. "These gods are complete morons. They are worse than us."

"Perhaps they are," Glimworm says. "Personally, I am not a fan of gods. They create life for the sole purpose of their own amusement. They wish to live through those they create. We are just a game to them. They give us conflicts and they give us gifts, all for the sake of entertainment."

"But not all gods could be this way," Delvok says. "Just our players."

"This is the only purpose a god has for creating life," Glimworm says. "If you had the power to create a world what would be your reason for doing it? Surely, it wouldn't be for the benefit of those who you create for your world. You would do it only for your own benefit, as a form of entertainment. A world is nothing more than a hobby to the god who creates it."

"So you think the god of the players created them only for his own amusement?" I ask.

"Perhaps," he says. "Maybe not for his amusement, but the amusement of his friends. Perhaps their god is just a Dungeon Master not unlike Aaron Donnelly. And he has gathered a large group of his friends together to play a game of Cubicles & Mortgage Payments. Perhaps Aaron, Mark, and Buzz are just player characters being roleplayed by some other beings from another world."

"Maybe," Loxi says. "But at least their Dungeon Master doesn't suck as bad as ours."

As we walk through the room, Itaa quickens her pace to catch up to me, hopping over sleeping gnolls. She takes my hand in hers, not at all embarrassed by who sees us together. Relationships between certain races are incredibly taboo in most cultures of our world. Goblins are especially xenophobic, but so are elves and dwarves. As I look over at Itaa, she smiles at me and blushes. When a goblin girl blushes, her cheeks turn a darker shade of green.

Loxi catches my eyes and giggles. She giggles in a way that is kind of demeaning, as if she thinks it's so cute that we're acting like we're in love with each other. As if the love between a goblin and a halfling could never truly be real love, similar to the way that two young children who say they are boyfriend and girlfriend could never truly be love.

I'm not exactly sure if I am in love with Itaa, nor am I sure that she is in love with me, but if we were I don't know why it would be considered a joke. It doesn't make the love any less real. But, I don't know, maybe she's right. Maybe it is funny and unrealistic for us to actually try to pursue a relationship. Maybe it is just cute and silly, in the way that it would be cute and silly if a cat was in love with a dog. I doubt goblins could mate with halflings. Although goblins are warm-blooded, they lay eggs like reptiles. Our physiologies probably just don't mix. Not to mention my people would never allow a goblin into their society, just as the goblins would never allow me into theirs.

Still, holding Itaa's hand feels nice. It's warm and soothing. Perhaps it would be impossible for a relationship between us to last, but I'm going to just go with it for now and see what happens. It is not likely that both or either of us will actually survive this quest anyway. I shouldn't worry about the future.

"So what is your plan?" Delvok asks the kobold wizard.

Glimworm winks at him. "Let's just say the line between fantasy and reality is about to become blurred."

23: Obelisk Room

We enter a great sanctuary glowing with white light. This chamber is different from all those in the rest of the dungeon, as if it were a part of a completely different castle. No, from a completely different world. It is a place of godly magnificence, with walls made of crystal and diamond, glimmering pearl pillars, and glass floors and ceilings that reflect the divine light all around us.

In the center of the room there is a magical obelisk, that slowly turns in its place. It radiates with sparkling blue energy and almost sings to us like a distant heavenly choir.

A group of figures stand before us, between us and the obelisk. They are five **level 6 paladins (AC -2, THAC0 14, hp 33, 42, 46, 49, 51, #AT 1, DMG two-handed swords +5, 1d10+5)** in fullplate armor +1.

"Damn," Glimworm says. "The Dungeon Master is trying to stop us."

"If you leave this room you will not be harmed," says

one of the paladins.

Glimworm leans over to me and says, "The Dungeon Master doesn't want us anywhere near that obelisk. He just wants you to continue on the quest he intended for you."

"What do we do?" I ask.

"Don't worry." Glimworm says. "Paladins are always of lawful good alignment. They won't attack us if we don't attack them."

The paladins raise their swords and attack us.

"I thought they wouldn't attack us?" I ask, as the paladins race toward us.

"I guess the Dungeon Master doesn't care!" Glimworm says. "Run!"

We scatter. The paladins split up and come after us.

"Don't bother trying to fight them," Glimworm yells out to us as he runs across the glowing glass floor. "Their armor class is nearly impenetrable!"

Delvok runs wildly from a paladin who has a sword raised above his head ready to hack down the elf. "And they have two-handed swords +5! Even if I had full hit points they could kill me in just one blow!"

Loxi decides to stop running and slash one chasing her with her broad sword. She misses, but the paladin does not. She loses 12 hit points, nearly all she had. She turns to run. The paladin gets a free hit, but narrowly misses. If he landed a blow she would have died instantly.

"We just need to insert the dildo into the obelisk," Glimworm yells at us. "The obelisk will do the rest."

Glimworm tosses me the dildo and I go for the obelisk. It is a good thing the paladins don't have a very high movement rate due to their heavy armor. If they were to have worn something a little lighter we would be dead already. The paladin chasing me won't be able to catch me before I insert the dildo.

The paladin on Itaa's tail sees me going for the obelisk

and breaks off his pursuit of her. He comes at me from the other side of the obelisk, cutting me off. With no way to reach the obelisk without taking on two paladins from two sides, I decide to toss off the dildo. Since Itaa is wide open now, I decide she's the right person to give it to.

"Itaa!" I scream to her, as I cut left away from the paladin in my path. "Catch!"

As I lead the paladins away from the obelisk, I toss the dildo at her like a football. She turns around just in time to catch it, but then she runs off in the opposite direction.

"No, Itaa," I yell. "Go for the obelisk!"

She just screams in panic, running frantically toward the far end of the room. "Itaa hate paladin!"

"Put the dildo in the obelisk!" I cry.

"Abadicks?" she yells.

Now she's just running in circles around a pillar with nobody following her.

"The big pointy thing in the middle of the room," I yell.

She sees the obelisk and goes toward it. Then all five of the paladins go after her. When she sees the gang of clanking armored men charging her, she screams and changes direction.

"Boobelf take!" Itaa cries, tossing the dildo to Loxi. "Itaa no want!" Then she gets as far away from the elf as she can.

"Oh, you little green bitch," Loxi says as the paladins come after her.

I get to the obelisk and hold my hands up. "Over here!"

Loxi tosses the dildo over the paladins' heads and it lands on the floor by my feet. I pick it up and point it at the obelisk.

"Where does it go in?" I ask Glimworm as he comes toward me.

The paladins also come toward me. All five of them raise their swords to attack. But Glimworm gets to me first. He takes the dildo out of my hand and pushes me back.

In an annoyed tone, he says, "Where do you think?"

Then I notice a glowing blue vagina on the side of the obelisk.

"That's just stupid," I say.

Glimworm rolls his eyes before he nods. "Tell me about it."

Just as the first paladin swings his 2-handed sword +5 at us, the kobold wizard stuffs the Dildo of Enlightenment +2 into the vagina. Then both of us duck and the paladin's sword bounces off of the side of the obelisk.

The room explodes with blue light. It shines so brightly that all of us fall to our knees and cover our eyes, even the paladins.

When the light dissipates, three figures appear in the room where the obelisk once stood: **Buzz Jepson (AC 10, THAC0 20, hp 6 #AT 1, DMG 1-2), Mark Meador (AC 9, THAC0 20, hp 4 #AT 1, DMG 1-2),** and **Aaron Donnelly (AC 10, THAC0 20, hp 8 #AT 1, DMG 1-2).**

All of our mouths drop open when we see them. Our players and the Dungeon Master are here, in the flesh, standing right in front of us. It takes a while for the three teenagers to realize what has happened to them. They look around the room, look at us, completely bewildered.

The paladins cease their attack and back away, not sure what to make of these newcomers. They failed in their mission to prevent the dildo from entering the obelisk, so they aren't quite sure what they should do, especially now that the Dungeon Master is no longer in the real world controlling their thoughts and actions. Now that he is with us, he is no longer the Dungeon Master. He is just like us, another character in our world. He doesn't control anybody anymore.

All the people in our entire world are probably in a state of confusion right now. For the first time in their lives, they have all gained freewill. Their thoughts are their own. Their actions are their own. They don't need a Dungeon Master anymore in order to exist.

"What the hell is going on?" Aaron yells, his voice whiney with panic, shaking in his wheelchair. "Where the fuck are we?"

Mark and Buzz are too shocked to even speak.

Glimworm steps forward.

"How does it feel, Dungeon Master?" Glimworm says to Aaron. "How does it feel to be inside of the world you created?"

"Who are you?" Aaron cries.

Aaron's double chin quivers as Glimworm approaches him.

"Don't you recognize your creations?" the kobold asks. "I am Glimworm, one of the many NPCs you created." Then he turns to Buzz and Mark. "And you two surely know Polo and Delvok. You rolled them yourselves."

As he looks around at us, the Dungeon Master begins to believe him. He realizes he actually is inside of the game he created.

"This isn't possible," Aaron says. "It was just a joke. The Dildo of Enlightenment, the obelisk, being aware that you guys were only characters in a roleplaying game . . . Those were all jokes!"

Glimworm says, "Ha. Ha. Ha. Yes, our whole world is just a joke to you. Our lives are nothing more than a pastime for you to amuse yourselves with."

"I didn't know!" Aaron says.

The kobold sticks his scaly muzzle into Aaron's face. "I'm going to enjoy ripping you to shreds."

I step forward. "Wait a minute . . ."

Glimworm looks at me.

"You're planning to kill them?" I ask.

A look of terror crosses the kids' faces.

"Of course," Glimworm says. "That's the only way to guarantee our freedom. We must kill our masters."

One of the paladins steps forward.

"We cannot allow you to kill these defenseless humans," says the paladin.

"You do not understand," Glimworm says. "You lawful good paladins protect the innocent, but you are destroyers of evil. Yes?"

The paladin nods.

"Well, these teenagers are far from innocent," Glimworm says. "All the evil that has ever happened in our world was created by them. They are responsible for countless murders, rapes, thefts, tortures, you name it. Because of this, these boys are far from lawful good."

Glimworm pulls out his dagger and points it at Aaron's neck. Then he says, "Based on their crimes in this world, I would say that the alignment of these boys is . . ." Then he turns and looks at the paladins. "Chaotic evil!"

The paladins look at each other, shrug, and turn away. They won't stand up for anyone of chaotic evil alignment and prefer not to even be in the same room with them.

"Then you should bring them to trial for their crimes," says the paladin.

"Yes, yes of course," the kobold says, nodding his head rapidly. "That is exactly what we plan to do."

"Good," says the paladin.

Then he turns to the other paladins and they nod their heads. They decide to leave the job of bringing these chaotic evil humans to justice in our hands, then they depart. The sound of clanking metal armor can be heard echoing through the crystal walls as they leave the room.

"Now," Glimworm says, turning back to Aaron, "I think we will bring you to trial. However, we will have to be your jury *and* your executioners." He turns to our group. "So, who thinks these boys deserve to be put to death for their crimes?"

"I do," Loxi says.

Of course, the assassin would want them dead.

"No, please!" Buzz cries. "Don't kill us!"

"It's not our fault!" Aaron says.

Glimworm nods at Loxi and says, "And I do, too, of course. They should die."

He turns to Delvok and asks for his vote.

"No, Delvok!" Buzz cries. "I created you. You can't kill me. It wouldn't be logical!"

Delvok sneers when he hears the word logical. He gives

his player a dirty look, like he wants to cut his heart out or beat him senseless. But then he tosses his sword on the ground. The sound of metal against the glass floor rings in our ears.

"I will not kill them," he says.

"Thank you!" Buzz cries. "I knew you were on my side!"

Glimworm's face fills with disgust. "What?"

"They are kids," he says.

"But they are monsters," says the kobold. "The biggest monsters our world has ever known. They deserve to die."

"I apologize," Delvok says, raising his hands. "But I cannot vote to kill them."

"Fine," Glimworm says, then he looks at me. "What about you?"

"No," I say, looking at Mark Meador as he stands paralyzed in his shoes. "I think we should just let them go. I think forcing them to live the rest of their lives in this crappy world they created is punishment enough."

"Damn!" Glimworm says, kicking the ground.

The players begin to relax.

"The goblin gets the final vote," Loxi says. "It's up to her."

We all look at Itaa. She is staring down the players and growling fiercely, her dagger in one hand, bow in the other.

"Who here speaks goblin?" Glimworm says. "Because I don't."

He looks at Loxi, but she shakes her head.

"I speak goblin," I say.

"Ask for her vote then," Glimworm says.

I nod.

"Itaa," I call to her.

She continues staring down the players, growling.

I say in goblinese, "Itaa, we are trying to take a vote to decide if we should kill them or let them live. I think you should vote to let them live. That's what I did."

"No," Itaa says.

She doesn't look at me, just growls at them.

"No?" I ask.

She says, "Itaa want kill three. Itaa eat three livers."

"Are you sure?" I ask. "They are just kids."

She points at Aaron. "Itaa start with Fatwheeler."

"What did she say?" Glimworm asks.

"She votes that they should live," I say.

Loxi rolls her eyes. "Bull. Shit."

"That's what she said," I say.

"Look at her," Loxi says. She points at Itaa to prove her point. The goblin is growling fiercely, ready to rip out their guts. "There's no way she said she wants to let them go."

"That's what she said," I say.

Glimworm shakes his head. "We can't trust the interpreter. We're going to have to translate the goblin's vote properly."

Loxi sighs and steps back. "I can't believe this shit. Let's just kill them and get it over with."

"Not a problem," Glimworm says to Loxi. "I have a scroll of **Read Languages**. We just need her to write out her vote and then it will be decided."

"Fine," she says.

As the kobold digs through his belongings, I step closer to Mark Meador.

"I'm sorry," I tell him, quietly. "I don't know if I can get you out of this."

Mark steps forward.

"It's really you, isn't it?" he says. "You're just as I imagined you to be."

I nod. "Well, you're just as I imagined you, too."

"Polo Pipefingers," he says. "In the flesh. This is all so insane."

I agree with him.

"So what was it like?" he asks, opening up to me. "What was it like having sex with all those elf girls?"

I shrug at him. "Not bad, I guess." But I don't tell him that it's sometimes annoying.

"You're so lucky," he says.

"It's not like I had a choice," I say.

"Oh yeah, sorry about that." He pauses and looks at his feet. "You know, if I ever would have known you were, you know . . . real, I never would have put you through all of those things."

"Yeah," I say. "I'm sure you wouldn't have."

"You're not going to let them kill me, are you?" he asks.

I look at the others. All of them but Delvok are thirsty for blood.

"I'll try my best," I say.

"Thank you," he says. "I think it would actually be really cool to explore this world. Maybe we could even go on quests together, me and you?"

"That would be weird," I say. "Questing with my player."

"And maybe we could have sex with some elf women!" he says, getting a little too excited all of a sudden.

"I don't know about that," I say. "I think I'm going to avoid elf sex for a while."

We laugh a little.

"No problem," he says. "But it would be cool if we could be friends."

I say, "Friends would be fine by me."

I hold out my hand and he shakes it.

"Yeah," he says, not letting go of my hand. "Best friends."

Then Itaa jumps on his back, wraps her arms around his shoulders, and screams into his ear.

"Itaa!" I yell at her.

Before Mark knows what's going on, the goblin cuts his throat with her dagger and blood sprays into my face. His four hit points bleed quickly out of him and his lifeless body falls to the floor.

"No!" I cry.

Itaa hops onto his dead chest and shouts, "Gothnerd deserve death for pain to Halfman. Itaa kill for Halfman!"

"I didn't want that," I say to her.

When they see their friend dead on the floor, Buzz and Aaron panic. Buzz drops to the ground and grabs the long sword Delvok tossed away, then he slashes at Loxi with it.

"The fuck!" she says, as the sword whips past her mohawk.

Then she stabs her broadsword through his stomach and he collapses into her giant elf boobs, covering her naked torso with his blood.

Aaron spins his wheelchair around and speeds away in the opposite direction, screaming at the top of his lungs, his cloak flapping behind him. Buzz still has one hit point left. He pulls himself off of Loxi's sword and out of her cleavage, then runs after Aaron, staggering as fast as he can while the blood pours down his legs.

"Don't let them get away," Glimworm cries.

The teenagers run to the south side of the room. They are doomed. There's nowhere out that way. Delvok and I stay back with Glimworm, but Itaa and Loxi chase after them. They are far behind them, but it doesn't matter. They'll catch up to them once they reach the dead end.

But on the other side of the room, Aaron immediately finds a secret door. Of course he would know where that was. He created this dungeon. He knows where everything is.

"You can't escape!" Glimworm yells.

The kobold wizard casts **Fireball** at them and the southern side of the room goes up in flames. Itaa and Loxi fall backward, dodging the explosion, but Buzz isn't so lucky. The Trekkie kid is swallowed by the fireball, burning away his last hit point.

Aaron, on the other hand, makes it through the secret door just in time. He speeds on his wheelchair through the corridor, laughing hysterically in triumph, as a wall of flames follows close behind him.

When the fire clears, we find Buzz Jepson's blackened corpse in the middle of the room. However, we also find the blackened corpses of seven naked wizards. They must have

I'm going to LARP
the FUCK out of you!

been invisible in this room the whole time, masturbating to Loxi's boobs, and were accidentally burned down by the Fireball spell.

"The Dungeon Master escaped," Glimworm says, moving toward the exit. "Let's get him."

Loxi and Itaa rush after him through the secret door.

I look at Delvok and then we look down at our dead players. We sigh at each other. It's strange to know that our gods, our creators, have just died in front of us. I'm glad that my destiny is in my own hands now, but their deaths just don't sit well with me. What bothers me most is that I'm kind of happy to see them dead. It also bothers me that I thought it was really cute how Itaa cut my player's throat like that. What the hell's wrong with me?

"We should follow the others," Delvok says.

I agree and we run toward the secret door.

30: Entry to the Catacombs

When we enter this room, we see the others looking around. There's no sign of Aaron. He's disappeared into the catacombs.

"Which way?" Loxi says.

There are three different directions.

"We should split up," Glimworm says.

Itaa is pacing back and forth stabbing the air with her dagger, chanting, "Kill Fatwheeler! Kill Fatwheeler!"

Then they hear Aaron's wheelchair echoing through the cavern to the east. We can also hear maniacal laughter.

"That way!" Glimworm says.

And we run toward the sound of his snorts and giggles.

37: Tomb of the Dead

Aaron is in his wheelchair on the other side of this room. He isn't running away, he's facing us, laughing madly at us.

"You can't kill me!" he screams. "I'm the Dungeon Master!"

Loxi runs toward him.

"Don't try it!" Aaron shouts at her. For some reason, that makes her stop. "I'm still in control here!"

Then he pulls out a tray from his arm rest and reaches into his pocket. He pulls out his special set of dice, the gold-plated set that cost him nearly $200 at Dragon*Con.

"I summon skeletons!" he says.

Then he rolls all of his dice at once on the tray of his wheelchair.

"This many!" he says.

He pulls out a notebook as he counts the total number from the dice. He writes down the number and says, "76 of them!"

I lean toward Glimworm and ask, "Does he still have his Dungeon Master abilities?"

Aaron looks around the room, waiting for the skeletons to appear.

"No," Glimworm says, shaking his head. "He just thinks he does."

"Take that you weaklings!" he cries, then he turns around and speeds off on his wheelchair to the next room, laughing at the top of his lungs.

"The little shit's gone mental," Loxi says.

We go after him.

38: Crypt

As we enter this room, we hear Aaron's voice but we don't see him.

His voice says, "You enter a dark, damp crypt. There are eight coffins lined into two rows in the center of the room. You hear the sounds of rats squeaking and gnawing on human remains. What do you do?"

We walk into the room, examining the coffins, searching for the kid. I rub against one of the coffins as I pass it.

We hear the sound of dice rolling.

"Oh no!" Aaron says. "Polo Pipefingers springs a trap!" We hear more dice rolling. "He failed his dexterity roll!" Then he rolls again. "It causes 13 points of damage!"

No trap was really sprung. No hit points were actually lost. We hear his laughter and the sound of his electric wheelchair as he zooms toward next area.

39: Abandoned Tunnel

The ground is beginning to get rougher here and so Aaron's wheelchair isn't moving as fast as it was. He laughs with his head all the way back.

Itaa runs toward him with her dagger. She's able to catch up to him on the rough terrain.

"You can't hit me," Aaron tells the goblin, "for I have a Cloak of Displacement!"

He puts the hood of his cloak over his head, and then

wiggles his body around as if he is displaced.

"Does it work?" Loxi asks.

"No," I say. "It's not really a Cloak of Displacement. It's just a blue bed sheet with silver glitter glued along the edges."

Itaa swings at the Dungeon Master with her dagger. As she attacks him, Aaron continues wiggling and rolls the 20-sided dice.

"Your attack roll failed!" he says.

By coincidence, she did actually miss him, hitting the seat of his wheelchair instead.

He turns his wheelchair around and flees. Itaa chases after him and stabs at his chair with her dagger. Every time she attacks, Aaron rolls his dice. She misses every time.

"Ha!" he cries. "You can't touch me while I'm wearing my cloak!"

Then she stabs him in the arm with the dagger.

"Ow!" he cries.

He speeds away to the next area, the dagger still sticking out of his arm.

40: Dragon's Den

When we arrive in this room, Aaron's wheelchair is stuck in the mud. The wheels are spinning, but he's not getting anywhere. He's still chuckling like mad.

We watch as a **huge red dragon (AC -5, HD 20, hp 396, #Att 3, DMG 4d8+8/1d12+2)** enters from the south. This dragon is one of Aaron's creations, so it has a giant 30' long fire-breathing boner that takes up half the room.

The rest of us hide in the entryway of the cavern from a safe distance. The dragon is the most powerful creature I have ever seen. It has no business being in an adventure for levels 2-5, yet here it is. Only the most cruel or inept of Dungeon Masters would throw a creature of this strength at such low level characters.

The dragon roars as it stomps toward Aaron. It points his massive boner at the crippled kid. The penis is dark red with thick veins popping out of its sides. Where the pee hole would be there is a giant mouth. The penis roars and then ejaculates a cloud of flames at the ceiling.

Aaron laughs at the dragon.

"Oh yeah," he says. "Well, I cast **Meteor Swarm**!"

He rolls his dice.

"That's 128 points of damage!" he tells the dragon.

The dragon points its giant penis at him. The colossal member looms above him, blocking out the light.

"Now I hit you with my Elven Long Sword +135," he tells the dragon.

He rolls the dice. Then he pretends he's cutting through the dragon with a sword. He even makes his own sound effects for it.

The giant penis opens its mouth to reveal a cavern of fang-like teeth.

Aaron rolls for damage.

"You've lost another 200 hit points!" he says, cackling at the top of his lungs. "You got pwned, bitch!"

But when he looks up at the dick and peers into its great jaws, his laughter stops. He goes silent, staring into the deep shaft, shifting uncomfortably in his chair.

As the mouth widens around him, he picks up his dice and rolls them again. Then he rolls them again. Then again. But he doesn't look down to see the results of the rolls.

We watch from safety as the red dragon's penis eats the Dungeon Master whole, wheelchair and all. We can hear the kid screaming inside as the dick chews him up. Then there is silence. The penis spits out the mangled wheelchair. It flies across the room, smashing against the wall next to us. Then the penis swallows Aaron's pulverized remains down its bulgy red shaft toward the dragon's secondary stomach: its nutsack.

Before we share the same fate as our poor pathetic DM, we decide to get the fuck out as soon as possible.

39: Abandoned Tunnel

"Killed by his own retarded, perverted imagination," Loxi says, as we walk lethargically through the tunnel. "A suitable death for him, don't you think?"

"I don't know," I say. "I kind of feel bad for him. He was just a kid after all."

"But he was a total dork!" Loxi says.

I shrug my shoulders.

"Kids die every day," Glimworm says. "In our world and in theirs. But this kid's death will benefit everyone in our world, forever."

"So how does this work?" I say. "If the Dungeon Master created our world how will it exist without him?"

"He just gave birth to our world," Glimworm says. "A child lives on when its mother dies, so will our world."

"But what about the parts of our world that the Dungeon Master has yet to create? Will those parts never exist? If we go to areas of the map that were not imagined by our DM will they just be a landscape of blank graph paper?"

"I don't think so," Glimworm says. "When a mother gives birth to a child the child continues to grow on its own without the help of the mother. Perhaps the mother still serves as guidance throughout the child's development but without her the child can still grow by itself. As we speak, I bet our world is growing and expanding all on its own."

"I hope you're right," I say. "If the only towns and

characters to ever exist in our world are those that the DM invented on the few quests we've done then it would be a very small world to live within."

"That will not be the case," he says. "The Dungeon Master just planted the seed. It will grow into a vast universe. Perhaps it already has."

I look over at Itaa walking next to me. She seems energized by seeing the DM's death. She is licking my player's blood from her fingers.

"No more Fatwheeler," she says, snickering to herself.

"But I don't get one thing," I say. "Everything we did, every action, every encounter, was determined by a roll of the dice. Who will be rolling the dice now? "

"The cosmic dice will roll themselves," he says. "It's called random chance. Dice are not necessary for us to figure out how fast our wounds heal, how much damage our attacks deal, which monsters we will encounter, how long we can last during sex. These are all determined by chance, the cosmic dice. When we had a Dungeon Master reigning over our universe, his dice overruled the cosmic dice. It won't be that way anymore."

38: Crypt

Glimworm stops as in the middle of the crypt.

"This is where we part ways," he says. "I must return to my work."

He shakes everyone's hands, including Itaa's, though she doesn't seem to understand what handshaking is for.

"Today is the first day of your real lives," he says. "Live them well."

He turns to walk away, toward the path to the west.

"Oh, wait," he says. "I almost forgot."

He pulls out a bag of gold coins and tosses them at me.

"Payment for retrieving the Dildo of Enlightenment +2, as promised," he says. "Plus a little extra for helping me end the reign of the Dungeon Master."

I look at the gold, amazed to actually have received treasure. We hadn't found a single gold piece since we started this quest.

"And you've also got the experience points for completing the mission," he says.

"Experience points?" Delvok looks around. "Experience . . . holy shit!"

Loxi and I look at him.

"I did it!" he says. "I finally got enough experience points to level up!"

His face bursts with delight.

"I'm finally level 2!" he says.

level up !

"All four of your classes?" I ask.

"No," he says. "Just one. But still, though!"

"Which one?" Loxi asks.

"Cleric!" he says. "I'm now a level 1 ranger/mage/fighter and a level 2 cleric! I can't believe it!"

Delvok raises his fist in the air and howls in triumph. Then, while watching him jump up and down with joy, I realize that for the first time since I've known him he's actually showing emotion. He's actually happy. He's not acting like a Vulcan anymore. The influence his player had over his personality is beginning to fade.

The kobold wizard salutes us. Then he turns and walks away. While standing in the middle of the crypt, we wonder what we should do next. We've obtained freewill, so now we can make our own decisions. We get to decide what we do next.

"Now that Glimworm is not after us anymore," I say, "we don't have to earn enough money to get out of town. We're in the clear."

"So should we just go back to town?" Delvok asks.

"We could do that," Loxi says. "Or we can continue to explore the catacombs and see if we can't find that treasure chamber we were originally after."

Delvok and I look at each other.

"It's our decision now," Loxi says. "We can do whatever we want. Whether we make safe decisions or dangerous ones, it's our call."

We pause and think about it for a minute.

Then Delvok says, "I think we should go for it. Let's find that treasure chamber and return home with a million platinum pieces!"

"Hell yeah!" Loxi says. "Let's do it!"

I hold out my hands. "I don't know, guys. I think I'd rather regroup with some extra adventurers and try again later."

They boo me and give me the thumbs down.

"Come on, halfling," Loxi says, lightly punching me in the arm. "Keep exploring with us."

"Okay, fine," I say. "But just for a little while. If we run into anything too dangerous we should turn around go back."

"Deal," Loxi says.

So we continue deeper into the catacombs.

41: Skeleton Cave

In this room, we find three animated **skeletons (AC: 7, MV 12", HD 1, hp6, #AT 1, D 1-6)**. After we kill them, we search their coffins and obtain 10gp each.

"I think I might retire after this quest," I tell the others.

"Oh yeah?" Loxi says.

"I don't think adventuring is for me," I say. "Besides, I'm a halfling fighter. Halflings make horrible fighters."

"You could change classes," she says.

"But halflings can only be thieves and fighters," I say. "And I just don't have the agility or desire to be a thief."

"Who says halflings can only be fighters and thieves?" she says. "The Players Handbook?"

I blink a few times. "Yeah, I guess."

"Fuck the Players Handbook," she says. "Be whatever you want to be."

"Well, I always wanted to be a mage," I say.

"Then be a mage," she says.

"Really?" I say. "You think I can do that?"

"Sure, why not?" she says.

"Maybe I will." I nod my head at her, then say. "But, you know. I don't really want to be an adventuring mage. I want to just be a town mage. You know, using my magic to help people out around the village."

"Like how?"

"I don't know," I say. "I just feel like staying in one place for a while. Get married. Start a family. That kind of thing."

Loxi smiles and looks over at Itaa. The goblin is holding my hand, leaning her head against my arm while swinging a dead skeleton's leg bone around like a wand.

"Is she the one you're thinking of settling down with?" she says, a giggle under her voice. "You know that could never possibly work, right?"

"Yeah," I say, looking over at her and then lowering my eyes to the ground. "I know. She's not the one to do that with."

Then we continue on to the next area.

42: Ghoul Lair

Sitting in the center of this room, we encounter a **ghoul (AC: 6, MV 9', HD 2, hp 14, #AT 3, D1-3/1-3/1-6, plus paralyzation)**. Delvok uses his new level 2 cleric abilities to **Turn Undead** and the ghoul disappears down the stairs to the east.

"Yes!" he shouts, pumping his fist in the air.

We pat him on the back. He's finally useful for something.

Delvok's yelling is heard from beings in area 43. We can tell by the excited screams of humanoid creatures echoing through the cavern in that direction. We go to investigate.

43: Goblin Lair

Upon entering this room, a party of seven **goblins (AC 7 HD 1-1, hp 7, 6, 5, 4, 4, 2, 2, #AT 1, D 1-6 or weapon)** charges us. Delvok and Loxi run into battle.

Itaa leaps between our party and the party of goblins. Both groups cease their attack.

"No kill!" she tells both groups. "Friends!"

Then I notice that these goblins have the same green tint to their skin as Itaa, the same striped tattoos. They must be from the same tribe. Itaa had said all of her people were enslaved or killed by the gnolls, but these goblins seem to have survived, hidden away in the catacombs all this time.

"Itaa still alive?" asks a male goblin, stepping forward.

When Itaa sees him, her jaw drops open.

"Yurtin?" she says, confused.

"Yurtin thought Itaa dead!" Yurtin cries, running to her. He hugs her to his green chest.

"Clan lives," she says. "Itaa thought clan no more."

The goblin kisses her, but she dodges his kiss to look back at me. His lips press against her cheek and don't let go. She separates herself from Yurtin and goes to me. "Are they your family?" I ask her.

"Itaa clan," she says, nodding her head.

"Is that your boyfriend?" I ask.

"Before, yes," she says. "Itaa thought Yurtin dead."

"Do you still love him?" I ask.

She pauses for a moment.

"Itaa love Yurtin," she replies, but she says it in a very sad voice.

I put my hand on her shoulder.

"You should stay with your people," I say. "You belong with them."

She looks up with a sad face, then nods. "Itaa belong with clan."

She looks at her people, then back to me.

"What if Itaa stay with Halfman?" she asks.

"I don't know," I say.

"Does Halfman . . ." she pauses on a word, her yellow eyes opening wide, "Does Halfman . . . *love* Itaa? Like Itaa love Halfman?"

I look up at the goblins and over at my friends. They are all staring at us, making me uncomfortable. But Itaa doesn't seem to care that we have an audience. She wants to hear my answer.

"I think I do," I tell her.

She smiles at me. When I smile back, she embraces me, causing the other goblins to gasp. Yurtin, her ex-boyfriend or perhaps he's even her mate, steps forward in response to the affection, almost ready to attack.

"Itaa not supposed to like Halfman," she says, separating us before we start a war. "Itaa sad to let Halfman go."

I nod at her and look at the ground between us.

"Itaa must stay," she says. "Itaa supposed to stay with clan. Itaa and Halfman no mix."

"I know," I say. "It could never work out."

"Itaa sad," she says.

"Polo sad, too," I say.

We stare at each other for a minute. I pat her on the head. Then she turns and goes to her people, looking back at me as Yurtin takes her into his arms.

I go back to my friends. When I see Loxi's expression, it almost looks apologetic. Even though she can't speak goblin, I think she could tell exactly what we were talking about.

"Are you okay?" Delvok asks.

"It's no big deal," I say. "We only just met. It's not like we were really in love or anything. That would be ridiculous."

I look down as a tear slips from my eye.

Loxi puts her hand on my chin and pulls my face up to hers.

"Polo," she says. "I think I was wrong."

"What do you mean?" I say, wiping the tear from my cheek.

She says, "I told you halflings and goblins can't be together. But that's bullshit. You can do whatever you want to do."

I shake my head. "It's okay. You're right."

"Fuck that," she says. "If you're in love with a goblin then be with a goblin. You have freewill now. You can do whatever the fuck you want."

"No," I say. "It would be a disaster."

I look over at Itaa. She's still staring back at me as Yurtin takes her away. It's probably for the best that she go with her people. If she stayed with me she'd probably always regret it. We would grow to hate each other or she'd end up getting killed by some racist cavalier when I wasn't around to protect her. No, she's better off with her kind. We'll forget all about each other soon enough.

But I can't just let her leave like this. I have to say something to her. A proper goodbye.

I step forward. I don't know what else to say, so I just say, "Halfman love Itaa!"

Itaa's eyes light up when she hears me say that, a wide smile crosses her face. She wiggles out of Yurtin's grasp, scratching and hissing at him until he lets her go. Then she runs at me.

"Itaa love Halfman!" she says, with her arms outstretched.

My mouth hangs open when I realize what I've just done. I probably should have said something else.

She wraps her arms around me and kisses me deeply, then kisses my cheek and my neck, and squeezes me to her as tight as she can.

"Itaa stay with Halfman," she says, excitedly. "Halfman understand Itaa. Halfman love Itaa."

I look her in the eyes and her wild pointy-toothed smile scares me a little bit.

"Are you sure?" I ask. "Won't you be happier with goblin-kind?"

She looks back at her people, then back at me.

"Itaa no know happy," she says, a tear falling down her green cheek, "until Itaa meet Halfman."

Then she kisses me again.

Behind her, the goblin tribe looks very upset. Some of them draw their swords. I'm not sure if they are angry at me, Itaa, or all of us.

She kisses me again, then says, "Itaa stay with Halfman forever!"

I realize there's no going back now. We're going to stay together.

I nod at her. "We'll make it work. We'll figure out a way."

The goblins approach us with their swords. They are growling and spitting. All of them are in an uproar. Yurtin steps forward and pounds his chest at me. I have no idea what's going on.

"One thing," Itaa says, looking back at her people. "Halfman must kill Yurtin."

My eyes widen. "What?"

"It way of Itaa clan," she says. "Halfman and Yurtin fight to death to win Itaa as mate."

Yurtin flexes his green muscles at me and roars.

"Oh," I say. "Fuck."

42: Ghoul Lair

I'm covered in blood and large wounds as we return to this room. The fight with Yurtin was brutal, but I managed to defeat him and get out of there with several hit points remaining. Itaa almost looked too pleased to see me cut off her ex-boyfriend's head. I'm going to have to learn to live with the fact that goblins love bloodshed. I'm sure her diet will also be something I'll have to deal with. As we walk across the room, Itaa is smiling and jumping up and down, her arms wrapped around my neck.

She cries, "Halfman win Itaa! Halfman win Itaa!"

Yeah. Halfman win Itaa.

She snuggles her bald head against the side of my neck, purring like a hairless green kitty cat.

What the hell have I gotten myself into?

"So where do we go from here?" Loxi asks. "Should we go back the way we came or take the stairs leading down to the east?"

"Those stairs lead off the map," Delvok says. "That is an area that had yet to be created by the Dungeon Master."

"Should we test Glimworm's theory?" I ask. "Should we see if the world is expanding itself?"

"Or do the stairs just lead into nothingness?" Delvok asks.

"I think we should try and see," Loxi says.

"But what if there's nothing there?" I ask. "What if we just disappear from this world the second we leave the map?"

"We'll never know until we find out," Loxi says.

We all agree.

I take Itaa by the hand and smile at her nervously. The four of us don't speak to each other as we continue to the next area. We take every step very slowly, cautiously, our eyes focused on what lies ahead, as we descend the staircase into the freshly birthed sections of our world.

the end

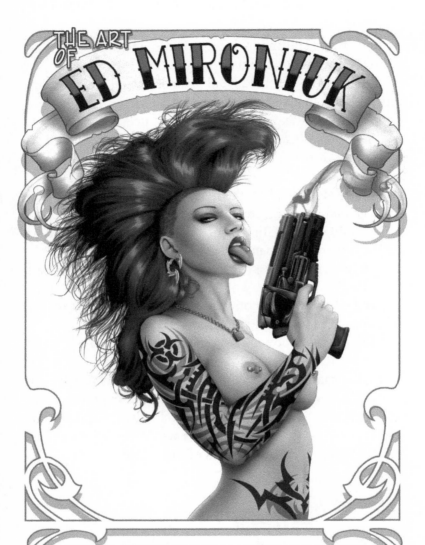

Author's Name: Carlton Mellick III	
Character's Name: Rocklar the Mighty	
Race: Half-Orc	
Class: Barbarian Warlord	
Level: 20	
Alignment: Chaotic Neutral	
THAC0: 1	
Height: 7'5 **Age:** 32	
Weight: 380 lbs **Sex:** M	
Hair: brown **Eyes:** steel	

HIT POINTS	ARMOR CLASS
132 / 132	5

ATTRIBUTES

STR 25	Attack Adj. +3	Damage Adj. +6	Weight Allow 3,000	Open Doors 50	BB/LG 40%
DEX 8	Reaction Adj. 0	Defense Adj. 0	Move Silently ✗	Hide in shadows ✗	
CON 17	Hit Points Adj. +3	Shock Survival 97%		Resurrection Survival 98%	
INT 2	Languages 0	Learn Spell Chance ✗		# of Spells Per Lvl ✗	
WIS -5	Magic Attack Adj. -8	Spell Bonus ✗		Chance of Spell Failure ✗	
CHA 0	Max # henchmen 0	Loyalty Base ✗		Reaction Adj. ✗	

	current xp	xp for next lvl
Experience Points:	2,300,000 /	2,500,000

BOOKS

Satan Burger, Electric Jesus Corpse, Sunset with a Beard, Teeth and Tongue Landscape, Steel Breakfast Era, Baby Jesus Butt Plug, Fishy-fleshed, Menstruating Mall, Ocean of Lard, Punk Land, Sex and Death in Television Town, Sea of the Patchwork Cats, Haunted Vagina, War Slut, Sausagey Santa, Ugly Heaven, Adolf in Wonderland, Ultra Fuckers, Cybernetrix, Egg Man, Apeshit, Faggiest Vampire. Cannibals of Candyland, Warrior Wolf Women of the Wasteland.

EQUIPMENT

Sideburns of Ogre Strength +5, a totally awesome skull necklace that shoots fireballs and shit, battle axe of destruction + 8 (+ 12 vs doppelgangers, + infinity vs you), glasses of seeing clearly, a cool Iron Maiden wallet that I got at the state fair in 1987, a 10'pole, a warhammer, some fancy cheeses, some beer.

GP: 1

AUTHOR BIO

CM3 is a powerful barbarian of the written word. While he might lack talent and a basic understanding of the English language, he makes up for this with sheer brute force. It is a known fact that the only reason anyone publishes him at all is because if they don't they'll get a fucking battleaxe through the face. While he has read a book or two in the past, he gets most of his inspiration from awesome movies like Hawk the Slayer and Beast Master 2.

WEBSITE

WWW.CARLTONMELLICK.COM

Introduce yourselves to the bizarro genre and all of its authors with the Bizarro Starter Kit series. Each volume features short novels and short stories by ten of the leading bizarro authors, designed to give you a perfect sampling of the genre for only $5 plus shipping.

BB-0X1
"The Bizarro Starter Kit"
(Orange)

Featuring D. Harlan Wilson, Carlton Mellick III, Jeremy Robert Johnson, Kevin L Donihe, Gina Ranalli, Andre Duza, Vincent W. Sakowski, Steve Beard, John Edward Lawson, and Bruce Taylor.

236 pages $5

BB-0X2
"The Bizarro Starter Kit"
(Blue)

Featuring Ray Fracalossy, Jeremy C. Shipp, Jordan Krall, Mykle Hansen, Andersen Prunty, Eckhard Gerdes, Bradley Sands, Steve Aylett, Christian TeBordo, and Tony Rauch.

244 pages $5

BB-001 **"The Kafka Effekt" D. Harlan Wilson** - A collection of forty-four irreal short stories loosely written in the vein of Franz Kafka, with more than a pinch of William S. Burroughs sprinkled on top. **211 pages $14**

BB-002 **"Satan Burger" Carlton Mellick III** - The cult novel that put Carlton Mellick III on the map ... Six punks get jobs at a fast food restaurant owned by the devil in a city violently overpopulated by surreal alien cultures. **236 pages $14**

BB-003 **"Some Things Are Better Left Unplugged" Vincent Sakwoski** - Join The Man and his Nemesis, the obese tabby, for a nightmare roller coaster ride into this postmodern fantasy. **152 pages $10**

BB-004 **"Shall We Gather At the Garden?" Kevin L Donihe** - Donihe's Debut novel. Midgets take over the world, The Church of Lionel Richie vs. The Church of the Byrds, plant porn and more! **244 pages $14**

BB-005 **"Razor Wire Pubic Hair" Carlton Mellick III** - A genderless humandildo is purchased by a razor dominatrix and brought into her nightmarish world of bizarre sex and mutilation. **176 pages $11**

BB-006 **"Stranger on the Loose" D. Harlan Wilson** - The fiction of Wilson's 2nd collection is planted in the soil of normalcy, but what grows out of that soil is a dark, witty, otherworldly jungle... **228 pages $14**

BB-007 **"The Baby Jesus Butt Plug" Carlton Mellick III** - Using clones of the Baby Jesus for anal sex will be the hip sex fetish of the future. **92 pages $10**

BB-008 **"Fishyfleshed" Carlton Mellick III** - The world of the past is an illogical flatland lacking in dimension and color, a sick-scape of crispy squid people wandering the desert for no apparent reason. **260 pages $14**

BB-009 **"Dead Bitch Army" Andre Duza** - Step into a world filled with racist teenagers, cannibals, 100 warped Uncle Sams, automobiles with razor-sharp teeth, living graffiti, and a pissed-off zombie bitch out for revenge. **344 pages $16**

BB-010 **"The Menstruating Mall" Carlton Mellick III** - "The Breakfast Club meets Chopping Mall as directed by David Lynch." - Brian Keene **212 pages $12**

BB-011 **"Angel Dust Apocalypse" Jeremy Robert Johnson** - Meth-heads, man-made monsters, and murderous Neo-Nazis. "Seriously amazing short stories..." - Chuck Palahniuk, author of Fight Club **184 pages $11**

BB-012 **"Ocean of Lard" Kevin L Donihe / Carlton Mellick III** - A parody of those old Choose Your Own Adventure kid's books about some very odd pirates sailing on a sea made of animal fat. **176 pages $12**

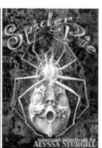

BB-013 **"Last Burn in Hell" John Edward Lawson** - From his lurid angst-affair with a lesbian music diva to his ascendance as unlikely pop icon the one constant for Kenrick Brimley, official state prison gigolo, is he's got no clue what he's doing. **172 pages $14**

BB-014 **"Tangerinephant" Kevin Dole 2** - TV-obsessed aliens have abducted Michael Tangerinephant in this bizarro combination of science fiction, satire, and surrealism. **164 pages $11**

BB-015 **"Foop!" Chris Genoa** - Strange happenings are going on at Dactyl, Inc, the world's first and only time travel tourism company.

"A surreal pie in the face!" - Christopher Moore **300 pages $14**

BB-016 **"Spider Pie" Alyssa Sturgill** - A one-way trip down a rabbit hole inhabited by sexual deviants and friendly monsters, fairytale beginnings and hideous endings. **104 pages $11**

BB-017 "The Unauthorized Woman" Efrem Emerson - Enter the world of the inner freak, a landscape populated by the pre-dead and morticioners, by cockroaches and 300-lb robots. **104 pages $11**

BB-018 **"Fugue XXIX" Forrest Aguirre** - Tales from the fringe of speculative literary fiction where innovative minds dream up the future's uncharted territories while mining forgotten treasures of the past. **220 pages $16**

BB-019 "Pocket Full of Loose Razorblades" John Edward Lawson - A collection of dark bizarro stories. From a giant rectum to a foot-fungus factory to a girl with a biforked tongue. **190 pages $13**

BB-020 "Punk Land" Carlton Mellick III - In the punk version of Heaven, the anarchist utopia is threatened by corporate fascism and only Goblin, Mortician's sperm, and a blue-mohawked female assassin named Shark Girl can stop them. **284 pages $15**

BB-021**"Pseudo-City" D. Harlan Wilson** - Pseudo-City exposes what waits in the bathroom stall, under the manhole cover and in the corporate boardroom, all in a way that can only be described as mind-bogglingly irreal. **220 pages $16**

BB-022 **"Kafka's Uncle and Other Strange Tales" Bruce Taylor** - Anslenot and his giant tarantula (tormentor? fri-end?) wander a desecrated world in this novel and collection of stories from Mr. Magic Realism Himself. **348 pages $17**

BB-023 **"Sex and Death In Television Town" Carlton Mellick III** - In the old west, a gang of hermaphrodite gunslingers take refuge from a demon plague in Telos: a town where its citizens have televisions instead of heads. **184 pages $12**

BB-024 **"It Came From Below The Belt" Bradley Sands** - What can Grover Goldstein do when his severed, sentient penis forces him to return to high school and help it win the presidential election? **204 pages $13**

BB-025 "Sick: An Anthology of Illness" John Lawson, editor - These Sick stories are horrendous and hilarious dissections of creative minds on the scalpel's edge. **296 pages $16**

BB-026 "Tempting Disaster" John Lawson, editor - A shocking and alluring anthology from the fringe that examines our culture's obsession with taboos. **260 pages $16**

BB-027 "Siren Promised" Jeremy Robert Johnson - Nominated for the Bram Stoker Award. A potent mix of bad drugs, bad dreams, brutal bad guys, and surreal/ incredible art by Alan M. Clark. **190 pages $13**

BB-028 "Chemical Gardens" Gina Ranalli - Ro and punk band Green is the Enemy find Kreepkins, a surfer-dude warlock, a vengeful demon, and a Metal Priestess in their way as they try to escape an underground nightmare. **188 pages $13**

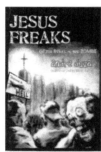  

BB-029 "Jesus Freaks" Andre Duza - For God so loved the world that he gave his only two begotten sons… and a few million zombies. **400 pages $16**

BB-030 "Grape City" Kevin L. Donihe - More Donihe-style comedic bizarro about a demon named Charles who is forced to work a minimum wage job on Earth after Hell goes out of business. **108 pages $10**

BB-031 "Sea of the Patchwork Cats" Carlton Mellick III - A quiet dreamlike tale set in the ashes of the human race. For Mellick enthusiasts who also adore The Twilight Zone. **112 pages $10**

BB-032 "Extinction Journals" Jeremy Robert Johnson - An uncanny voyage across a newly nuclear America where one man must confront the problems associated with loneliness, insane dieties, radiation, love, and an ever-evolving cockroach suit with a mind of its own. **104 pages $10**

BB-033 **"Meat Puppet Cabaret" Steve Beard** - At last! The secret connection between Jack the Ripper and Princess Diana's death revealed! **240 pages $16 / $30**

BB-034 **"The Greatest Fucking Moment in Sports" Kevin L. Donihe** - In the tradition of the surreal anti-sitcom Get A Life comes a tale of triumph and agape love from the master of comedic bizarro. **108 pages $10**

BB-035 **"The Troublesome Amputee" John Edward Lawson** - Disturbing verse from a man who truly believes nothing is sacred and intends to prove it. **104 pages $9**

BB-036 **"Deity" Vic Mudd** - God (who doesn't like to be called "God") comes down to a typical, suburban, Ohio family for a little vacation—but it doesn't turn out to be as relaxing as He had hoped it would be... **168 pages $12**

BB-037 **"The Haunted Vagina" Carlton Mellick III** - It's difficult to love a woman whose vagina is a gateway to the world of the dead. **132 pages $10**

BB-038 **"Tales from the Vinegar Wasteland" Ray Fracalossy** - Witness: a man is slowly losing his face, a neighbor who periodically screams out for no apparent reason, and a house with a room that doesn't actually exist. **240 pages $14**

BB-039 **"Suicide Girls in the Afterlife" Gina Ranalli** - After Pogue commits suicide, she unexpectedly finds herself an unwilling "guest" at a hotel in the Afterlife, where she meets a group of bizarre characters, including a goth Satan, a hippie Jesus, and an alien-human hybrid. **100 pages $9**

BB-040 **"And Your Point Is?" Steve Aylett** - In this follow-up to LINT multiple authors provide critical commentary and essays about Jeff Lint's mind-bending literature. **104 pages $11**

BB-041 **"Not Quite One of the Boys"** **Vincent Sakowski** - While drug-dealer Maxi drinks with Dante in purgatory, God and Satan play a little tri-level chess and do a little bargaining over his business partner, Vinnie, who is still left on earth. **220 pages $14**

BB-042 **"Teeth and Tongue Landscape"** **Carlton Mellick III** - On a planet made out of meat, a socially-obsessive monophobic man tries to find his place amongst the strange creatures and communities that he comes across. **110 pages $10**

BB-043 **"War Slut"** **Carlton Mellick III** - Part "1984," part "Waiting for Godot," and part action horror video game adaptation of John Carpenter's "The Thing." **116 pages $10**

BB-044 **"All Encompassing Trip"** **Nicole Del Sesto** - In a world where coffee is no longer available, the only television shows are reality TV re-runs, and the animals are talking back, Nikki, Amber and a singing Coyote in a do-rag are out to restore the light   **308 pages $15**

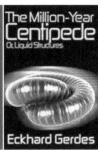

BB-045 **"Dr. Identity"** **D. Harlan Wilson** - Follow the Dystopian Duo on a killing spree of epic proportions through the irreal postcapitalist city of Bliptown where time ticks sideways, artificial Bug-Eyed Monsters punish citizens for consumer-capitalist lethargy, and ultraviolence is as essential as a daily multivitamin. **208 pages $15**

BB-046 **"The Million-Year Centipede"** **Eckhard Gerdes** - Wakelin, frontman for 'The Hinge,' wrote a poem so prophetic that to ignore it dooms a person to drown in blood. **130 pages $12**

BB-047 **"Sausagey Santa"** **Carlton Mellick III** - A bizarro Christmas tale featuring Santa as a piratey mutant with a body made of sausages. 124 pages $10

BB-048 **"Misadventures in a Thumbnail Universe"** **Vincent Sakowski** - Dive deep into the surreal and satirical realms of neo-classical Blender Fiction, filled with television shoes and flesh-filled skies. **120 pages $10**

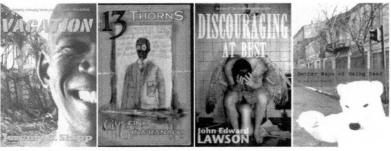

BB-049 **"Vacation" Jeremy C. Shipp** - Blueblood Bernard Johnson leaves his boring life behind to go on The Vacation, a year-long corporate sponsored odyssey. But instead of seeing the world, Bernard is captured by terrorists, becomes a key figure in secret drug wars, and, worse, doesn't once miss his secure American Dream. **160 pages $14**

BB-051 **"13 Thorns" Gina Ranalli** - Thirteen tales of twisted, bizarro horror. **240 pages $13**

BB-050 **"Discouraging at Best" John Edward Lawson** - A collection where the absurdity of the mundane expands exponentially creating a tidal wave that sweeps reason away. For those who enjoy satire, bizarro, or a good old-fashioned slap to the senses. **208 pages $15**

BB-052 **"Better Ways of Being Dead" Christian TeBordo** - In this class, the students have to keep one palm down on the table at all times, and listen to lectures about a panda who speaks Chinese. **216 pages $14**

BB-053 **"Ballad of a Slow Poisoner" Andrew Goldfarb** Millford Mutterwurst sat down on a Tuesday to take his afternoon tea, and made the unpleasant discovery that his elbows were becoming flatter. **128 pages $10**

BB-054 **"Wall of Kiss" Gina Ranalli** - A woman... A wall... Sometimes love blooms in the strangest of places. **108 pages $9**

BB-055 **"HELP! A Bear is Eating Me" Mykle Hansen** - The bizarro, heartwarming, magical tale of poor planning, hubris and severe blood loss... **150 pages $11**

BB-056 **"Piecemeal June" Jordan Krall** - A man falls in love with a living sex doll, but with love comes danger when her creator comes after her with crab-squid assassins. **90 pages $9**

BB-057 **"Laredo" Tony Rauch** - Dreamlike, surreal stories by Tony Rauch. **180 pages $12**

BB-058 **"The Overwhelming Urge" Andersen Prunty** - A collection of bizarro tales by Andersen Prunty. **150 pages $11**

BB-059 **"Adolf in Wonderland" Carlton Mellick III** - A dreamlike adventure that takes a young descendant of Adolf Hitler's design and sends him down the rabbit hole into a world of imperfection and disorder. **180 pages $11**

BB-060 **"Super Cell Anemia" Duncan B. Barlow** - "Unrelentingly bizarre and mysterious, unsettling in all the right ways..." - Brian Evenson. **180 pages $12**

BB-061 **"Ultra Fuckers" Carlton Mellick III** - Absurdist suburban horror about a couple who enter an upper middle class gated community but can't find their way out. **108 pages $9**

BB-062 **"House of Houses" Kevin L. Donihe** - An odd man wants to marry his house. Unfortunately, all of the houses in the world collapse at the same time in the Great House Holocaust. Now he must travel to House Heaven to find his departed fiancee. **172 pages $11**

BB-063 **"Necro Sex Machine" Andre Duza** - The Dead Bitch returns in this follow-up to the bizarro zombie epic Dead Bitch Army. **400 pages $16**

BB-064 **"Squid Pulp Blues" Jordan Krall** - In these three bizarro-noir novellas, the reader is thrown into a world of murderers, drugs made from squid parts, deformed gun-toting veterans, and a mischievous apocalyptic donkey. **204 pages $12**

BB-065 "Jack and Mr. Grin" Andersen Prunty - "When Mr. Grin calls you can hear a smile in his voice. Not a warm and friendly smile, but the kind that seizes your spine in fear. You don't need to pay your phone bill to hear it. That smile is in every line of Prunty's prose." - Tom Bradley. **208 pages $12**

BB-066 "Cybernetrix" Carlton Mellick III - What would you do if your normal everyday world was slowly mutating into the video game world from Tron? **212 pages $12**

BB-067 "Lemur" Tom Bradley - Spencer Sproul is a would-be serial-killing bus boy who can't manage to murder, injure, or even scare anybody. However, there are other ways to do damage to far more people and do it legally... **120 pages $12**

BB-068 "Cocoon of Terror" Jason Earls - Decapitated corpses...a sculpture of terror...Zelian's masterpiece, his Cocoon of Terror, will trigger a supernatural disaster for everyone on Earth. **196 pages $14**

BB-069 "Mother Puncher" Gina Ranalli - The world has become tragically over-populated and now the government strongly opposes procreation. Ed is employed by the government as a mother-puncher. He doesn't relish his job, but he knows it has to be done and he knows he's the best one to do it. **120 pages $9**

BB-070 "My Landlady the Lobotomist" Eckhard Gerdes - The brains of past tenants line the shelves of my boarding house, soaking in a mysterious elixir. One more slip-up and the landlady might just add my frontal lobe to her collection. **116 pages $12**

BB-071 "CPR for Dummies" Mickey Z. - This hilarious freakshow at the world's end is the fragmented, sobering debut novel by acclaimed nonfiction author Mickey Z. **216 pages $14**

BB-072 "Zerostrata" Andersen Prunty - Hansel Nothing lives in a tree house, suffers from memory loss, has a very eccentric family, and falls in love with a woman who runs naked through the woods every night. **144 pages $11**

BB-073 **"The Egg Man" Carlton Mellick III** - It is a world where humans reproduce like insects. Children are the property of corporations, and having an enormous ten-foot brain implanted into your skull is a grotesque sexual fetish. Mellick's industrial urban dystopia is one of his darkest and grittiest to date. **184 pages $11**

BB-074 **"Shark Hunting in Paradise Garden" Cameron Pierce** - A group of strange humanoid religious fanatics travel back in time to the Garden of Eden to discover it is invested with hundreds of giant flying maneating sharks. **150 pages $10**

BB-075 **"Apeshit" Carlton Mellick III** - Friday the 13th meets Visitor Q. Six hipster teens go to a cabin in the woods inhabited by a deformed killer. An incredibly fucked-up parody of B-horror movies with a bizarro slant. **192 pages $12**

BB-076 **"Rampaging Fuckers of Everything on the Crazy Shitting Planet of the Vomit At smosphere" Mykle Hansen** - 3 bizarro satires. Monster Cocks, Journey to the Center of Agnes Cuddlebottom, and Crazy Shitting Planet. **228 pages $12**

BB-077 **"The Kissing Bug" Daniel Scott Buck** - In the tradition of Roald Dahl, Tim Burton, and Edward Gorey, comes this bizarro anti-war children's story about a bohemian conenose kissing bug who falls in love with a human woman. **116 pages $10**

BB-078 **"MachoPoni" Lotus Rose** - It's My Little Pony... *Bizarro* style! A long time ago Poniworld was split in two. On one side of the Jagged Line is the Pastel King-dom, a magical land of music, parties, and positivity. On the other side of the Jagged Line is Dark Kingdom inhabited by an army of undead ponies. **148 pages $11**

BB-079 **"The Faggiest Vampire" Carlton Mellick III** - A Roald Dahl-esque children's story about two faggy vampires who partake in a mustache competition to find out which one is truly the faggiest. **104 pages $10**

BB-080 **"Sky Tongues" Gina Ranalli** - The autobiography of Sky Tongues, the biracial hermaphrodite actress with tongues for fingers. Follow her strange life story as she rises from freak to fame. **204 pages $12**

BB-081 **"Washer Mouth" Kevin L. Donihe** - A washing machine becomes human and pursues his dream of meeting his favorite soap opera star. **244 pages $11**

BB-082 **"Shatnerquake" Jeff Burk** - All of the characters ever played by William Shatner are suddenly sucked into our world. Their mission: hunt down and destroy the real William Shatner. **100 pages $10**

BB-083 **"The Cannibals of Candyland" Carlton Mellick III** - There exists a race of cannibals that are made of candy. They live in an underground world made out of candy. One man has dedicated his life to killing them all. **170 pages $11**

BB-084 **"Slub Glub in the Weird World of the Weeping Willows" Andrew Goldfarb** - The charming tale of a blue glob named Slub Glub who helps the weeping willows whose tears are flooding the earth. There are also hyenas, ghosts, and a voodoo priest **100 pages $10**

BB-085 **"Super Fetus" Adam Pepper** - Try to abort this fetus and he'll kick your ass! **104 pages $10**

BB-086 **"Fistful of Feet" Jordan Krall** - A bizarro tribute to spaghetti westerns, featuring Cthulhu-worshipping Indians, a woman with four feet, a crazed gunman who is obsessed with sucking on candy, Syphilis-ridden mutants, sexually transmitted tattoos, and a house devoted to the freakiest fetishes. **228 pages $12**

BB-087 **"Ass Goblins of Auschwitz" Cameron Pierce** - It's Monty Python meets Nazi exploitation in a surreal nightmare as can only be imagined by Bizarro author Cameron Pierce. **104 pages $10**

BB-088 **"Silent Weapons for Quiet Wars" Cody Goodfellow** - "This is high-end psychological surrealist horror meets bottom-feeding low-life crime in a techno-thrilling science fiction world full of Lovecraft and magic..." -John Skipp **212 pages $12**

ORDER FORM

TITLES	QTY	PRICE	TOTAL

Please make checks and moneyorders payable to ROSE O'KEEFE / BIZARRO BOOKS in U.S. funds only. Please don't send bad checks! Allow 2-6 weeks for delivery. International orders may take longer. If you'd like to pay online via PAYPAL.COM, send payments to publisher@eraserheadpress.com.

SHIPPING: US ORDERS - $2 for the first book, $1 for each additional book. For priority shipping, add an additional $4. INT'L ORDERS - $5 for the first book, $3 for each additional book. Add an additional $5 per book for global priority shipping.

Send payment to:

BIZARRO BOOKS
  C/O Rose O'Keefe
  205 NE Bryant
  Portland, OR 97211

Address

City   State   Zip

Email   Phone

Lightning Source UK Ltd.
Milton Keynes UK
UKHW010639230820
368696UK00001B/28